Bolan froze as subtle movement drew his attention to the trees

The red badge clipped to the lapel of the soldier's fatigue shirt marked him as a member of Doyle's team. He had to have traveled hard to get that far in the amount of time that had elapsed, and traveled quietly, as well.

The man was framed in the Executioner's sights, but he was reluctant to fire. Where were his teammates? It made no sense that the man would have come this far alone.

Something hissed past Bolan's face and struck the tree beside him. The soldier ducked, half expecting to be sprayed with paint, but splinters stung his flesh instead.

Live rounds!

The game had taken a bizarre and deadly turn. Someone had switched the paint rounds in his weapon for a standard killing load....

MACK BOLAN ®

The Executioner

DON PENDLETON'S
EXECUTIONER®
THE
PATRIOT GAMBIT

THE ★ AMERICAN TRILOGY BOOK 1

A GOLD EAGLE BOOK FROM
WORLDWIDE®

TORONTO • NEW YORK • LONDON
AMSTERDAM • PARIS • SYDNEY • HAMBURG
STOCKHOLM • ATHENS • TOKYO • MILAN
MADRID • WARSAW • BUDAPEST • AUCKLAND

First edition June 1997
ISBN 0-373-64222-9

Special thanks and acknowledgment to
Mike Newton for his contribution to this work.

PATRIOT GAMBIT

Patriotism is not a short and frenzied outburst of emotion, but the tranquil and steady dedication of a lifetime.

—Adlai Stevenson
1900-1965

The self-styled "patriots" who have injected violence into national politics are about to learn a hard lesson.

—Mack Bolan

To David North, a fallen warrior. God keep.

PROLOGUE

"Hey, look, we all know you're a Communist!"

"You don't know squat, my pointy-headed friend." Meyer Lowman leaned in closer to the microphone and watched the red lights flashing on his console, six more phone lines waiting to unload their daily dose of venom. "If you had a working brain, you'd know something, but what you've got inside that tiny skull of yours is petrified manure."

"Fuck you, Jew-boy!"

Lowman smiled. Lucille, in the control booth, would delete the expletives.

"That's beautiful," he crooned into the microphone. "You have your brown shirt on, I take it? All dressed up with nowhere to go? Did you know that half of Hitler's closest confidants were raving homosexuals?"

"You filthy—"

Lowman cut him off and glanced in the direction of the wall clock. Ten more minutes and his show was over for the day. It didn't matter if the calls were backed up all the way to Canada. Come 2:00 p.m., the Super Jew was history.

One of the wags around the station had been first to tag him, and the label stuck, as much because Lowman liked it as for any other reason. He wasn't religious—hell, he hadn't been to synagogue in at least twelve years—but it was something friends and enemies alike could fixate on, promote the show by word of mouth.

And if he stopped to think about it, Lowman would admit there were more enemies than friends out there in Radioland. What of it? Ratings mattered, and it made no difference whether listeners were tuning in to curse him or to kiss his ass. As long as they kept tuning in—and *phoning* in—Meyer Lowman would be rated number one among the local crop of shock jocks, and he could hold out for bigger money when his contract was negotiated in the spring.

It was a game, of course, but there were times when it got to him all the same. He hadn't known there were this many neo-Nazi types in Billings before he started taking on-air potshots at right-wing religious hucksters and their paramilitary cronies. Before that he was just another talking head, too ugly for the boob tube, running third behind a women's program and an aging Bircher who was still hyped up about the plot to fluoridate Montana's drinking water. What he needed was a hook, and Lowman had found it thirteen months earlier, the day a mush-mouthed member of the tiny Billings KKK had phoned in to expound his views on human evolution.

It had been a massacre.

To this day Lowman doubted that the Klansman understood what Meyer was saying to him, but it made no difference. Others heard him loud and clear, some calling in to praise his nerve, while a larger number phoned to give him hell, denounce his politics, his parentage, whatever they could think of in the name of "real Americans."

Lowman loved it. He had found his niche.

The station owner thought about it for a day or so, considered firing him, then took a look at the ratings and decided that he loved it, too. The price of advertising on Lowman's show began to climb, and he was on his way.

There had been threats, but that was normal. He had received a few *before* the show turned controversial. One note, scribbled with a crayon in those dear, long-ago days, had promised to see him dead for putting such a dull show on the air.

Nobody said that anymore.

It was a stepping-stone, of course. From Billings he was on his way to bigger, better things.

Lowman fielded another call, then said, "Hey, hey! We're out of time!" and left the booth.

His station was on Rimrock Road, in northern Billings, with a fenced-in parking lot next door. The day was clear and cool as the DJ stepped into early-autumn sunshine, moving toward his car. He drove a Mazda now, but it would be a BMW one day soon, no doubt about it.

In radio jargon he was number one with a bullet.

An aging security guard held the gate for him, waving him through, and Lowman nodded in passing. Be nice to the little people on your way up, he always said—or the little people who counted, at least—because they would be right there, waiting for you, on your way down.

He took his time, driving with the windows down, relieved as always that he got off work before the rush hour. There was time for a couple of beers at his favorite watering hole, on Poly Drive, before he made his way back home to Susan.

"Hey, Super Jew!"

The voice came from his left, a bit behind him, closing fast. Lawman checked the mirror, saw a slice of fender and he turned to glance in the direction of the voice. He saw the automatic weapon and just had time to think *Oh, shit!* before the world exploded in his face.

THE BOMB WAS PERFECT. It was like a miracle, Buzz Reilly thought, the different recipes you could whip up with ordinary things around the house and garden. There was homemade napalm, for example: mix your gasoline and laundry soap just right, and it would stick to anything—or anybody. Same thing with your basic fertilizer, if you knew what you were doing.

Reilly did.

He might have flunked his junior year in high school, but no one in that school had ever learned to motivate him. He was motivated now, for damn sure, and he got his lessons right the first time, every time.

He had been experimenting with different recipes for months now, wondering if he would ever get a chance to use his skill for real. Now that it was time, he almost had to pinch himself to realize his dream was coming true. The bastards who had always kept him down, made fun of him—his lisp, red hair, the way he walked—could all go straight to hell.

It was a great responsibility to build the bomb *and* drive the truck. That showed how much his brothers trusted him. It made Buzz Reilly proud. He wouldn't let them down, no matter what he had to sacrifice to carry out his mission.

There was no rush driving over to the courthouse. They had told him half a dozen times to take it slow and easy, watch the speed limit and not give the blue-suits any lame excuse to stop him. Just in case, he had a phony driver's license, used to rent the truck, but that could blow up in his face if someone checked it through the state-police computer system.

If it came to that, Reilly was prepared to use the Astra A-100 semiauto pistol slung beneath his left arm in a horizontal shoulder rig. It was a .40-caliber, just like the FBI men carried. He had practiced long and hard to draw and to hit a man-size target at a range of twenty feet. Up close, like reaching through the driver's window with his registration papers, Reilly figured there was no way he could miss.

He had to forget that now. He had a more important job to do, delivering the payload right on time. Speaking of time, the detonator wasn't primed yet, just in case he hit a snag in traffic. It was simple, not unlike a kitchen timer. When he got the truck in position, all he had to do was to give the knob a twist, then lock the cab and take a hike. His backup would be waiting for him two blocks from the courthouse, in a stolen car.

Reilly saw the courthouse now, and felt a new sense of excitement building inside him. This was it, the moment he had trained for, waited for since he was just a little kid, a chance to hit back at the world and do some good for the United States at the same time.

He had to laugh, sometimes, the way shit happened.

Eighteen months earlier, if anyone had asked him about blowing up the main courthouse in Wichita, he would have reckoned they were crazy, maybe high on something. Not that Reilly would have turned them in by any means, but neither would he have been anxious to participate. That's where the education helped, filling the blank spots in his mind with knowledge of the vast conspiracy that stretched from Washington and Moscow, all around the world.

The people of America were waiting for a wake-up call, and Reilly was about to dial their number, let it ring out loud and clear. He would be damned by all the brainwashed drones who thought their lives were perfect, sucking on the federal tit and letting Uncle Sammy tell them when to wipe their ass, but that would change in time.

Besides, they wouldn't know who pulled it off. Not Reilly's name, nor the militia's. That was part of a guerrilla war, he realized. Spread havoc and confusion through the enemy encampment, while the righteous warriors hung out with their trusted friends.

And for the first time in his life, Buzz Reilly had some friends, the kind who would protect him when the shit came down. That was another miracle, damn right.

The courthouse had security assigned to watch the parking lot. You had to be a government employee or a juror to proceed beyond the checkpoint, but he didn't need to get that close. The side street, Waco Avenue—sweet irony—was good enough. He had already scouted it and knew about the fifteen-minute loading zone, orange curb and all.

Reilly reckoned fifteen minutes would be long enough.

The space was empty. He nosed the truck toward the curb, switched off the engine and pocketed the keys. He could dispose of them at leisure, once he got away from there. The payload's firing mechanism filled a shoebox, just within his reach behind the driver's seat. The rest of the device was bulky plastic barrels packed with sudden death.

He gave the timer's knob a twist, past twenty minutes to engage the gears, then brought it back until the arrow rested on fifteen. All done, he locked the driver's door behind him, lit a cigarette while he was crossing at the corner.

The car was waiting for him, just as Reilly knew it would be.

"So, how'd it go?" Alex asked as Reilly took the shotgun seat.

"It went," Buzz said. "Let's roll."

THE ARMORED CAR was late, but only by a minute and a half, so there was no cause to worry yet. If anyone was wise, if they had changed the route, there would be uniforms all over Cody's team by now.

He couldn't help worrying. This was the mission that would make or break him with the brotherhood, prove his command ability or mark him as a loser. If he couldn't pull it off…

The walkie-talkie on the Plymouth's seat beside him hissed and sputtered. "Coming."

Just the one word. It was all he needed from their spotter to the north. The armored car was on its way, proceeding south on Highway 101. It was impossible to know exactly how much cash would be inside, but Cody understood the

average Monday-morning shipment to Ukiah ran between
three and four million dollars.

Not bad.

"Let's do it," Cody told the others, switching off the
safety on his Heckler & Koch 93 rifle and stepping from
the Plymouth. Four men followed him and took position
without speaking, each already crystal clear on what he had
to do. Another lookout, to the south, would warn them of
approaching traffic and use every means at his disposal to
prevent a rude surprise while they were taking down the
armored car.

Cody let Hicks and Schaefer handle the LAW rockets.
Any member of the team could use the little throwaway
bazookas, but they had drawn straws beforehand for the
honor. Kendrick took the east side of the highway with his
Barrett Model 82-A1. If there was any static from survivors
in the truck once it was stopped, the big .50-caliber weapon's armor-piercing rounds would keep the argument from
dragging on too long.

He waited, standing on the western shoulder of the highway with his automatic rifle, listening. A moment later he
heard the truck approaching. Ten or fifteen seconds more,
and it would be in view, emerging from the cover of a low
embankment on his left, just where the highway curved.

That curve had been a crucial part of Cody's plan. On
most of Highway 101, the driver would have seen them
waiting from a mile away. He could have radioed for help,
or simply turned around and left them standing in the middle of the road. This way Cody's commandos had the edge
surprise provided to a savvy warrior. By the time the driver
and his backup saw their danger, it would be too late.

"Here goes."

The curt announcement came from Schaefer, and Cody
saw the squat, gray armored car roll into view.

Any second now...

The rockets flew toward impact, one the slightest bit off

center, but it made no difference to the end result. They were designed for disabling tanks and other military vehicles. The armored car was like a toy compared to the M-1 Abrams battle tank. It took the hits and swerved hard left, the driver dead or losing it, and nosed into the roadside ditch.

So far so good.

Cody advanced, his rifle braced in one hand, while the other gripped a cardboard placard. He got close enough for anyone inside the cab to see him through the pall of engine smoke, and raised the sign. Its message, inked with a black marker, was succinct: Get Out Or Die.

At first he thought they might be dead already, then he figured one of them was trying out the radio. If they were getting through, if they could stall him long enough, it could get rough.

"Give them the fifty," he commanded.

Kendrick cranked off three rounds, their impact clanging on the steel plate beside the driver's door. A moment later someone cracked the double doors in back, smoke wafting out as if it were a giant oven and the roast was burned.

Three men in uniform emerged, making no resistance as their pistols were removed from holsters. Schaefer kept them covered with his Kalashnikov while Cody and the others ducked into the truck and started slinging sacks of money onto the pavement. Paper tags attached with wire told Cody how much money each blue bag contained, but he ignored them, grabbing everything he could and chucking it behind him, leaving someone else to stack it neatly on the roadside.

Kendrick brought up the Plymouth, and by the time the armored car was empty, Schaefer had begun to load the trunk.

Sweating underneath his ski mask, Cody left the armored car and turned to face his captives. "Back inside," he ordered.

They did as they were told and climbed back inside the hull of what had been their rolling fortress. Hicks stood next to Cody, facing the three uniforms, his Uzi leveled from the waist.

There was no signal, nothing to alarm the three men before a double stream of bullets ripped into their bodies, spinning them and dropping them in pools of blood.

"Let's go."

When Cody was back inside the Plymouth, he palmed the two-way radio and thumbed down the button. "We're out of here," he said.

There was no answer from the lookouts, north or south, but he hadn't expected one. They both had motorcycles hidden close at hand, and duffel bags to hold their weapons, once the guns were broken down. The spotters would be miles away before police arrived, and so would Cody's crew.

The hit had gone like clockwork. He was pleased.

It was a damn fine start, he told himself, but it was just a start.

The best was yet to come.

1

Mack Bolan held the Blazer to a steady sixty-five miles per hour, rolling south on State Road 287, through the heart of Madison County, Montana. Sheridan was already behind him, and the famous Robbers' Roost, where Butch Cassidy's Wild Bunch had once eluded Pinkertons and sheriffs' posses, was off to his left somewhere, a tourist exhibit these days. The curious could stop and see where bad men of another age had fought and died.

As the sun went down behind the Bitterroots, off to the west, the Executioner was more concerned with bad men of the present day. Not outlaws, in the normal sense, although they might have tried to claim some kinship with the spirit of those gunmen from a century gone by. The men he sought weren't afraid to rob and kill, by any means, but they had cloaked their crimes in politics and tried to hide behind Old Glory, something Cassidy had never thought of in his wildest dreams.

The next sign up put Laurin five miles down the road, and Bolan started to ease off the accelerator, slowing to forty as the settlement came into view. A town required at least two hundred residents to rate a listing in his road atlas, and Laurin didn't make the grade. It showed up on the map, all right, a fly speck, but you had to know what you were looking for and where to find it, since the index wasn't any help.

Laurin was one of countless tiny towns that dotted the

foothills of the Rocky Mountains, maybe once a mining camp or lumber mill, the old days gone and more or less forgotten now. Its children would be bused to school, most likely in Virginia City, until they were old enough to flee and seek their fortune in the larger world outside. A handful would return, but towns like Laurin never seemed to grow.

Except of late, the soldier thought, and watched the street signs, hoping that he wouldn't miss his destination and be forced to circle back. These days a few small towns in Idaho, Montana, Washington and other Western states were drawing people many of the old-time residents could gladly do without. Change wasn't always progress, as a wise man once proclaimed, and there were those who would have rather seen their town dry up and blow away than watch it grow by taking on "the wrong sort" from outside.

Back in the 1970s some tiny towns in northern California had experienced the same phenomenon. In those days the new settlers had been hippies, looking for a little slice of Eden in the cool Age of Aquarius, someplace where they could plant their marijuana seeds and maybe do a little chanting on the side. Tune in, turn on, drop out.

The hippies had grown up, but the idea of separation from society was still in vogue. Today, however, those who sought to make the break were typically a different breed. The hair might still be long, depending on religious quirks, but there was nothing of the easygoing seventies in their philosophy. The new exiles were militant, well armed, belligerent. Their politics fell somewhere to the right of Adolf Hitler, in the twilight zone of paranoia. Some of them lived in rural compounds, fortified against attacks by the Zionist Occupational Government—ZOG—in Washington, D.C. They often balked at paying taxes, posted warnings on their land that trespassers would be gunned down and generally behaved as if they lived within a state of siege.

And those were just the moderates.

Of late some groups had taken the defensive paranoia

one step further. They had gone on the attack, declaring open war on the United States.

Bolan spied a poster, stapled to a phone pole just ahead: Meeting Tonight! An arrow pointed off to Bolan's left. He turned into the next side street and slowed to a crawl.

It had to be the church. The place was all lit up, with people milling on the grass and steps outside. From what he saw on the approach, it didn't seem that all of them were locals. Clustered near a pair of vintage vans downrange, he counted eighteen men and women, mostly young, who didn't seem to fit the Laurin style. The women—girls, more like—wore mostly jeans and T-shirts, one or two in peasant skirts and blouses. Their male counterparts wore denim jackets with the sleeves cut off and blue jeans with the knees out, several sporting shades despite the darkness. Two or three of them were black, wearing dashikis over slacks, with brightly colored headwear.

Outsiders, Bolan thought, and there was no good reason to suppose they had come to listen quietly.

The paramilitary separationists hadn't gone unopposed, by any stretch. Aside from angry locals in the towns they colonized, their racist-sexist-homophobic propaganda had sparked outrage from minorities, and self-styled action squads had mobilized to follow "patriotic" speakers everywhere they went, disrupting rallies, swapping hatred with the best of them. When cooler heads could get a word in edgewise, they explained that hecklers, rock throwers and miniriots only gave the enemy more free publicity, but anger seemed to be the common currency in politics these days.

Sometimes the Executioner was moved to wonder what had happened to America. He remembered Vietnam, the protests, thousands chanting in the streets. Had the disintegration started then, or was it something much more recent, much more deadly?

In the old days, Bolan knew, the violent fringe in politics

had really *been* a fringe: perhaps a hundred college kids across the country who had liked to play with bombs, some bigots—white and black—who came to grief when they had tangled with the FBI. There was a time when all the nation's Klansmen, Weathermen and Panthers thrown together wouldn't fill a midsize auditorium.

But things had changed. A cold wind gusted through the heartland of America, and it was leaving bodies in its wake.

He found a place to park the Blazer, half a block west of the church, and walked back past the vans, across the street. His own garb—jeans, a sheepskin jacket and a chambray shirt—was more in keeping with the neighborhood, but he didn't intend to pass for a local. The Wyoming plates his Blazer wore came from a federal stash, and anyone who checked them out on the computer net would find his cover with supporting background data.

Bolan knew that he would have to do the rest of it himself.

In terms of hardware, he was almost naked, with a Bearpaw folding knife in snap-down leather on his belt. There was a shotgun in the Blazer, with his side arm and a shoulder rig, all hidden from the prying eyes of any uniforms who gave the vehicle a once-over. He had decided that it made no sense to go in packing, even if it multiplied his risk. The men he hoped to meet were constantly alert for spies and infiltrators. If they took him for an undercover cop, he would have lost before he ever got a chance to play.

In fact he might be dead.

The church was filling up when Bolan got there. No one tried to frisk him, but there were two guards on the door, eyeballing everyone who entered. The soldier would have liked to hang out on the steps and watch them greet the would-be hecklers, but he had to find himself a seat.

There was an empty spot halfway down, on Bolan's

right. A couple in their sixties scooted across to let him have the aisle, and he thanked them as he settled in.

The audience was rumbling quietly, the kind of noise you get from any crowd, a bit subdued at being gathered in a church. He looked around for uniforms and saw no evidence of cops or sheriff's deputies. The local lawmen either weren't expecting trouble, or else they preferred to wait and watch from outside the church.

The Executioner tapped into the conversations swirling all around him, picking up on snatches here and there. Some in the audience were mostly curious, he saw, but there were also those who muttered racial slurs or spoke about the FBI and ATF in bitter, scathing terms. United by a hatred of the octopus that spread its grasping tentacles from Washington, they had turned out to have their darkest fears confirmed, their anger validated.

Bolan checked his wristwatch. It was almost time.

He ran some mental demographics on the crowd while he was waiting for the show to start, and found that some four-fifths of the attending audience was male, with ages ranging from midtwenties to eighties. None of the women in the crowd were unescorted; mostly were wives, from Bolan's take, with the same hardbitten look as their men. If it had been the 1930s, he might have pegged the audience as Dust Bowl victims. In the present setting, though, it wasn't Mother Nature that had angered them.

A side door opened, off the dais, and three men emerged to stand in front of metal folding chairs lined up behind the pulpit. The first guy out of the gate was portly, middle-aged, with gray around the temples of his swept-back hair. The horn-rimmed glasses heightened his resemblance to a square, squat-bodied owl. He had a dog-eared Bible wedged beneath one arm, and looked as if he were about to take off charging toward some adversary's goalpost any second. Bolan made him as the preacher and moved on.

The second man in line was younger, slimmer, without

qualifying as athletic. He had put more thought into coordinating colors, suit and tie, than the minister had. He carried note cards cupped in one hand, reminding Bolan of a high-school student getting ready to present a valedictory address. His smile was bright and confident, and it seemed to take an effort for him not to raise his hand and wave to the assembled audience.

The last man through the door fell somewhere in between the other two in terms of age. He was the tallest of the three by several inches, and his ramrod bearing indicated military training somewhere down the line. His salt-and-pepper hair was buzzed down to the scalp, with shaggy brows providing shade for cobalt eyes. His square-cut jaw was marred on one side by a scar that ran fish-belly white between his left ear and the corner of his thin-lipped mouth.

He stepped up to the pulpit while his two companions sat. He tapped the microphone a few times with his index finger, satisfied with the reverberation, leaning slightly forward as he spoke.

"Good evening, patriots!" he said by way of introduction. "Some of you know me already. For the rest of you, I'm Colonel Ralph Pike of the Paul Revere Militia."

Roughly half the audience applauded that, the rest reserving judgment. No one whistled, given their surroundings, but a couple of the young bucks in the crowd looked as if they wanted to.

"It's good to see this kind of turnout on short notice," Pike continued, "and from a community the size of Laurin. Give yourselves a hand!"

Most of the audience was clapping now. Pike stood before the microphone, applauding *them* and smiling like a teacher who has found himself presented with a classroom full of budding geniuses.

"That's right!" he said, voice ringing out above the ripples of applause. "Community is what we're all about. The Paul Revere Militia is a movement of the people in America today, and that's got certain folks worried back in Washington. You know the ones I mean. They talk about equality and freedom, just before they stab you in the back and take your land away. You'll see them strike a pose on family values, while they're sending troops to crush God-fearing Christians with their tanks and jackboots. All that talk about protecting children, while they're passing condoms out in kindergarten and promoting homosexuals to run the schools. They want to take your guns away with one hand, while the other opens up those prison gates and lets the animals come out to play in your backyard!"

There was sustained applause this time, with several voices calling "Amen!" from the audience. So far the Executioner hadn't heard anything he couldn't get from any televangelist eight days a week.

"But hey," Pike said, "don't get me started, folks!"

That brought a laugh, as it was meant to do, the audience relaxing just a little, backing off from the ignition point. The basic message had been driven home, and there was no escaping it, whatever happened next.

"Tonight is not about the Paul Revere Militia," Pike informed them, lying through his straight white teeth. "Our literature will be available for those who care to read about the group, and I'll be happy to take any questions later on. Right now, I'm here to introduce a man of God who understands the Scripture like few men before him. More importantly he understands its application to the world we walk around in every day. He doesn't waste his time on humanistic 'social gospels' of the welfare state and godless communism. If you're looking for a mealy-mouthed evangelist with one hand out for money and the other begging for approval from the so-called cultural elite, you've come to the wrong place tonight, I kid you not!

"Now," Pike said, "without further ado, it's my honor and privilege to introduce the Reverend Alan Chalmers, representing Christ Our Lord's Cathedral of the Air. The Reverend Chalmers, ladies and gentlemen!''

Some members of the crowd were on their feet, a sporadic ovation that didn't quite catch on. Bolan kept his seat and watched the square man with the Bible in his hand approach the pulpit, grinning like a lottery winner as he scanned the audience. He left his fans standing for another moment, basking in the warmth of their applause, before he gestured for them to sit down.

''I thank you, brethren.'' Bolan was familiar with the high-pitched voice, since he'd checked out the preacher's act on video, but it was still incongruous, considering his bulk. ''And I would like to thank my Christian brother, Colonel Pike, for that outstanding introduction. I just hope I live up to his words of praise.''

This time the laughter was polite, restrained, almost perfunctory.

''You know,'' the preacher said, ''I asked the Lord last week if I should write a sermon for tonight, and he suggested that I speak directly from my heart instead, so that's what I intend to do. We're living in a time of trouble, friends. One nation under God has gone to hell while we were napping, and it's getting more hellacious by the day. You don't need me to tell you that. You've got your newspapers, your television and your common sense to show you what's been going on across America. We're living in an age of signs and wonders lifted straight from Revelation, pointing to a day when the elect of God will stand in battle ranks against the forces of the Antichrist and live or die according to their faith in him who made the world!''

Applause and plenty of ''Amens!'' erupted from the assembly. Bolan did his part and nodded earnestly while he was clapping, seeming perfectly at ease with what the preacher had to say.

''Our politicians talk no end about the need to save America,'' Chalmers said, ''but the trouble is that all most of them do is talk. Not all of them, praise God! I wouldn't go that far. In just a moment you'll be meeting one who puts his muscle where his mouth is. But I'm talking now about the ninety-nine-point-nine percent who sell their honor and their souls to gain positions of authority. The ones who promise anything and lie right to your face about the good they mean to do in Washington or in the state-house. Never mind which party they belong to, friends. We've been sold out by the Republicans and Democrats alike. The only difference is, one side pretends to be your bosom friends before they sell you down the river, while the other tells you right up front exactly what they mean to do.

"As far as I'm concerned, the bunch of them are two-bit gutless Judases, and when the day comes, Jesus Christ our Lord will send them all straight down to hell! Do not pass Go. Do not collect thirty pieces of silver!"

Most of the crowd was eating it up, a few of them frowning—though whether in anger or agreement with the preacher's words, Bolan couldn't be sure. He glanced back toward the doors that opened on the narthex and the street outside, in time to see the pointmen for the would-be hecklers hassling with security. The church was full already; they would have to stand if they got in at all, and Bolan wondered whether they had nerve enough to press the point.

The preacher's tone had softened somewhat by the time he spoke again, as the applause died down. "Things may look dark," he said, "but I'm obliged to tell you that there is good news tonight. There's hope. You heard me right. Our enemies outnumber us right now, and they control the seats of power in this land, but we have God behind us, and a few brave men who risk their lives to take his part.

"At this time I would like to introduce a man you folks here in Montana should be proud of. He's the new kid on the block in Washington, but he's already made his mark.

You know exactly where he stands on the important issues, and your opposition knows that, too. They've got him marked, make no mistake about it, and he needs your help to carry out his mandate from the last election. He can make a difference if you help him. Friends and neighbors, your own freshman congressman, Neal Martz!''

It was the young man's turn, and Bolan joined in the applause as he approached the pulpit, taking time to run down what he knew about the congressman. In office for eleven months, Martz voted with the conservative Republican block on most issues, but held himself aloof from any taint of compromise with the White House on economics, social-welfare programs, gun control—the whole nine yards. There was a rumor that the Speaker of the House considered Martz "reactionary," which was a glowing testimonial for most of his constituents. A maverick who had been accused of right-wing paranoia in the mainstream press, he had appeared in public with militia leaders during his campaign, and obviously didn't shun their company now that the office was his.

"My friends," Martz said through the applause, "it's my great pleasure to be here tonight and fill you in on what's been happening in Washington these past few months. I know the stories that you hear from sources in the media don't always jibe with the reality of government and how it will affect your daily life."

"Amen to that!" somebody called out from the audience, provoking laughter all around.

"I hope to cut through some of that malarkey if I can, and tell you what *I'm* doing to protect your interests in what used to be *our* nation's capital."

"Whose interests would those be?"

The question, shouted, came from somewhere near the entrance to the sanctuary. Bolan turned and saw that half a dozen of the activists whom he had seen outside were in the church now, their companions still encountering resistance from militiamen assigned to watch the door. The man who posed the question was a tall, dashiki-clad African-American, eyes hidden by the shades he wore, his goateed chin thrust out pugnaciously.

Behind the podium Neal Martz was smiling, taking it in stride. "My friend, if you'll identify yourself and tell us which part of my district you reside in, I'll be pleased to take your question."

"I'm not one of your pathetic peckerwoods," the black man said to rising murmurs from the crowd. "I represent the People's Freedom Coalition, as I'm sure you know."

Martz kept his smile in place. "I can't say I'm familiar with—"

"Oh, really? Could that be because you spend your time with redneck, racist, homophobic trailer trash out on the shooting range, instead of doing what you're sworn to do?"

By this time Colonel Pike was on his feet and pushing forward, toward the microphone. "If you don't like the First Amendment, boy—"

He got no further, as the other members of the heckling crew began to shout and jabber all at once, as if in answer to a signal they had arranged. The women seemed to favor shouted curses, while a couple of the men began to sing "We Are the Champions," and the rest made booing, hissing sounds. Outside the entrance to the sanctuary, fists were flying. Pike jumped off the dais and approached the heckling band with long, swift strides.

The smoke grenade came out of nowhere, hissing as it landed in the center aisle and started fogging up the room, its pop and sizzle drowned by angry shouts and female screams.

Mack Bolan didn't hesitate. He saw his chance and took it, lunging from his pew and straight into the middle of the fight.

2

The meeting went to hell in seconds flat. A second smoke grenade came hurtling from the knot of hecklers, landing near the podium.

Someone shouted, "Fire!"

A stampede for the exits was impeded by the wooden pews and grappling brawlers in the center aisle, where Pike had reached the leader of the jeering section, trading blows toe-to-toe.

The black guy would have held his own with most opponents, but he clearly didn't have Pike's military training in the martial arts, and it was showing in the way he staggered after taking hits. His guard was dropping.

Another pair of hecklers broke ranks, charging toward the colonel, one of them unlimbering a pair of homemade nunchakus from beneath his baggy shirt. Pike didn't see them coming in the smoky room, with people milling all around him, concentrated as he was on dealing with his first opponent. Bolan saw his opportunity and knew that he would be an idiot to let it pass him by.

He dodged around a pair of senior citizens, the old man brandishing a cane in one hand, clinging to his wife's arm with the other, grazing Bolan's shoulder with a mistimed blow. The Executioner stayed focused on his targets, passing Colonel Pike and his opponent, stepping in to meet his adversaries in the middle of the crowded aisle.

The man with the nunchakus saw him, wiping teary eyes

and blinking at the smoke as he reared back to swing his weapon. Bolan was about to go inside the swing, when a slender blonde ran in between them, looking for a way out of the crowd. The nunchakus made a hollow pop as they rebounded from her skull, and she lurched sideways, squealing as she fell against the nearest pew and tripped a forty-something farmer.

Before his adversary could recover, Bolan stepped in close and struck him with an open palm between the eyes, a straight shot from the shoulder, making sure to pull it short of lethal force, avoiding contact with the nose that would have driven splinters deep into the brawler's brain. It was enough to send him reeling backward, nunchakus slipping from his fingers as he staggered clear, his partner closing in to join the fight.

The attacker came empty-handed, firing off a roundhouse swing at Bolan's head that could have done some damage had it reached the target. Rather than waiting for the blow to fall, however, the soldier gripped the slugger's wrist and pivoted to lift him off his feet, a simple judo toss that put his adversary on the floor. From there it was an easy move to step across his straightened arm, still clinging to that captive wrist, and use the leverage needed to twist and dislocate his shoulder. Bolan dropped the wounded arm when his opponent screamed, and left him writhing on the floor.

A moment later Pike's assailant tripped across the fallen man and went down on his backside, fresh blood streaming from his nose and lips. Pike stepped in close to kick him in the face and finish it, then glanced up through the haze of drifting smoke at Bolan.

"Watch your back!" he snapped, and the soldier spun in time to meet the groggy nunchaku fighter, empty-handed now but coming back for more. His wild swing glanced off Bolan's shoulder, and the Executioner struck back with two swift punches to the gut, immediately followed by a jarring uppercut. His adversary folded like a rag doll, slumping to the floor.

"Which way, sir?" Bolan made a point of putting military deference in his tone as he addressed the colonel.

"Out the back," Pike answered. "Follow me!"

A glance back toward the narthex showed him bodies locked in combat, others surging toward the exit, jostling one another in their flight. Between him and the door, the aisle was filling up with bodies. Each time one of the casualties would try to rise, a fist or foot would slam him down again, or someone else would stumble, sprawling, adding to the crush.

Bolan followed Pike against the flow of bodies rushing toward the main doors of the sanctuary, elbowing the strangers right and left to forge a path between them. No one stood against him, but it was still a struggle, like swimming upstream in the rapids, with weights on his feet. He took repeated hits from heads, fists, elbows, knees, knowing he would be black and blue.

He scanned the smoky dais, but saw no sign of Congressman Martz or the preacher. They had bailed out while the getting was good, covered by smoke and Pike's leap from the stage to confront their assailants.

The door on Bolan's left led to the sacristy. Pike shouldered through, and the soldier followed, glancing back to see the sanctuary clearing, as the press of bodies gradually extruded to the narthex and the street outside.

The door swung shut behind him, cutting off the view, and Bolan brought his mind back to the path ahead. Pike seemed to know where he was going, and the Executioner thought they should be relatively safe once they had cleared the building. From the glimpse he'd had of their assailants, he couldn't picture any kind of major ambush waiting in the dark.

They didn't linger in the sacristy, but rather moved on through another, smaller room, and made their way outside,

Pike leading through what seemed to be a side door of the church. From where they stood, in darkness, Bolan couldn't see his Blazer or the crowd that produced so much angry, frightened noise from the direction of the street. There was a smallish house in front of him, protected by a chain-link fence and what appeared to be a cocker-poodle hybrid, leaping at the fence and snarling out of all proportion to its stunted size.

"This way," Pike said, and moved out toward the street on Bolan's right. Before they covered twenty feet, a siren wailed, and colored lights began to dance in storefront windows up and down the street.

"Police!" Pike hissed. "Goddammit!"

"Is there something wrong, sir?"

"Wrong?" Pike's face was otherworldly as he turned on Bolan, half in shadow, while the other half kept changing colors—red, blue, amber, white.

"The bastards set us up!" Pike said. "They must have had eyes in the crowd. Hell, those were probably their people with the smoke grenades. They'll stop at nothing. You should know that. If you're wise, you'll get out while you can."

"No, sir," the Executioner replied. "With all respect, I'll take my chances."

"What's your name?" He regarded Bolan with narrowed eyes.

"Belasko, sir. Michael J."

"All right, Michael J., let's go to work."

They ran around the street side of the church, Pike leading by a yard or so. A glance showed Bolan that his Blazer seemed to be untouched, still well outside the epicenter of the action, with the milling crowd, a few antagonists still brawling, uniforms unloading from their cars and closing in with riot sticks.

A hasty count of cars and badges startled Bolan. If he had been forced to guess at Laurin's law-enforcement population, he would have put his money on a marshal and a deputy or two, one car to share if they were lucky. Now he counted eight patrol cars parked at crazy angles in the street, each vehicle disgorging three or four tough-looking men in khaki uniforms. He knew that kind of force wouldn't show up in Laurin once a year in normal circumstances, and there hadn't been sufficient time to draw them from surrounding towns.

So Pike was right in one respect: the lawmen had been waiting for him when he got there. That was still a mighty leap of faith away from proving cops set up the miniriot, though. More likely, Bolan thought, the county sheriff was aware of the potential for disorder at militia gatherings and had decided to take out insurance.

Either way, however, it didn't fit Bolan's plans to see his quarry spend the night in jail, much less to join him in the tank. There had to be another way.

Pike was charging straight into the fray, arms sweeping startled dawdlers to the left and right, clearing a path. One of the agitators—male or female, Bolan couldn't say for sure in the confusion—blundered out in front of Pike and caught a swift punch in the face that flattened him or her.

The other fighting focused on the front doors of the church, where several of the colonel's bouncers were engaged with members of the rat pack that had broken up the meeting. Left alone, the home team would have ultimately been guaranteed a victory, but the police weren't prepared to let it go that far. In fact they were already wading through the crowd, a human wedge aimed toward the broad church steps and double-timing through the wall of bodies in their path.

Pike moved to intercept them, closing from the spearhead's flank, on a diagonal. "You have no business here, with your provocateurs!" he shouted as he closed the gap.

There was a chance the officers would have ignored him, but he grabbed one of them by the arm and tried to pull him out of line. At that the deputy lashed out with his baton, but Pike was quick enough to block the swing, retaliating with a quick punch to the ribs.

Two other cops were on him in a flash. Their comrades sized up the situation and decided three could handle it all right, and proceeded toward the main brawl on the front steps of the church. It was the opportunity Bolan had been waiting for, and he couldn't afford to let it pass.

One of the cops was rearing back to strike at Pike's head from behind when Bolan caught his wrist and used a sweeping kick to cut his legs from under him. Before he hit the ground, the deputy had already absorbed two lightning punches to the face, and he was out of it, his nightstick gripped in Bolan's fist.

Should he take time to grab the gun? he asked himself. No.

One of the deputies cracked Pike across the shins and brought him to his knees, the other cranking one of Pike's arms up and back until the colonel had to bow or sacrifice the shoulder joint. His head was slumping forward, bending toward the ground, when Bolan stepped in close and swung his captured stick against the nearest khaki elbow he could find.

The result was both dramatic and immediate. The startled deputy let out a howl of pain, released Pike's arm and swung around to face his unseen adversary. From the smooth, thick torso, Bolan knew the cop was wearing Kevlar underneath his shirt, but bulletproof and pain resistant were two very different things. Before his adversary could recover from the shock of impact to his elbow, Bolan stepped inside his guard and jabbed one end of the baton into his solar plexus.

Even with the vest, it was a jarring blow that rocked the deputy back on his heels, his round face coloring beneath the visor of his riot helmet. Bolan knew that it was futile to prolong the contest, with so many other uniforms close by. He followed with a low cut to the knee that set his target hopping, then finished with a backhand to the face that broke his nose.

"Freeze, asshole!"

Bolan froze from the neck down, head slowly turning toward the source of that command. The third cop had released his grip on Colonel Pike and drawn his service pistol, aiming it right-handed, while the left hand clung to his baton. It wasn't the ideal stance for a combat situation, but his target was essentially unarmed, no more than fifteen feet away and frozen in his sights.

Most people, in the circumstances, would have lost their concentration in a rush of panic, frightened for their lives. A few—the hardened criminals with nothing left to lose— would have attacked without a second thought, fighting to kill or be killed rather than go back to jail.

The Executioner did neither. He was lining up his angles, waiting, counting off the doomsday numbers in his head, when Pike reached up between those khaki thighs and grabbed a handful of the family jewels. He squeezed and twisted, using all the strength that he could muster, and the deputy forgot about his target as the pain exploded from his groin to drop a screen of white noise in his brain.

The nightstick flew from Bolan's hand and struck his adversary's wrist, the service pistol tumbling from numb fingers, barely noticed as it fell. He closed the gap with long, swift strides and slammed a fist into the mouth that had been opened wide to scream, without effect.

Three up, three down.

He helped Pike to his feet and drew him toward the street, away from the chaotic melee on the steps.

"My car, sir."

"Car?" Pike blinked his cobalt eyes back into focus, swiping at a crimson thread that ran between his hairline and his cheek. "Right! Lead the way, son!"

They were almost to the Blazer when a pair of civilians

came at Bolan out of nowhere. There was no time to recall
if he had seen them with the other members of the action
squad, around the van, but they were clearly of the same
persuasion, and they seemed to recognize the colonel.

"Pike!" one of them snarled. "You fascist bastard! This
is for the people!"

Drawing back to swing a sawed-off bat as he addressed
the enemy, the shaggy young man reckoned without Bolan's intervention. When the first blow slammed into his
ribs, he staggered, grunting with the pain, and changed his
target, lashing out at the Executioner with the bat.

All things considered, it wasn't the best defensive move
he could have made. Another heartbeat, and his wrist was
trapped in one strong hand, his arm extended, locking at
the elbow, while he felt himself drawn hopelessly off balance, to the front. An elbow slammed into his face with
enough force to snap off his incisors at the gums, and the
lights went out before he crumpled to the street without the
bat.

The snoozer's friend was having second thoughts, but it
was too late to cut and run. Instead, he dropped into a
crouch, fingers hooking into claws as he began to make a
moaning sound.

The style was new to Bolan, probably self-taught in front
of the TV, and he had no time left to fool around with
amateurs. He feinted with the bat, then lashed out with his
left foot in a kick that raked his adversary's knee. The leg
turned into rubber, any semblance of a fighting stance dis-
solving in a flash. Instead of going for the head shot, Bolan
swung his captured bat against the young man's collarbone
and left him thrashing in the street, trying to right himself
with one arm and one leg.

He used his key and slid behind the Blazer's steering
wheel, leaned over to unlock Pike's door and had the engine running by the time Pike settled in the shotgun seat.

"You did all right back there," the colonel said when

they had put two blocks between the miniriot and themselves.

"I've had some practice," Bolan replied. "Where to, sir?"

Pike drew a handkerchief and held it to the thin gash in his forehead. "I was riding with the preacher, but he didn't wait around. I've got no vehicle."

"You do now, sir."

He felt Pike watching him and kept his eyes fixed on the road. "You're not a local, are you?"

"No, sir."

"Those Wyoming plates for real?" Pike asked.

"That's where I started out," Bolan said. "You might say I'm in between engagements, sir."

"You have some military background. No mistaking that."

"Yes, sir. It's been a while."

"You've stayed in shape, though."

"Well, I haven't had much choice, sir."

"You done any time?" Pike asked.

He made a point of frowning, leaving the colonel to figure out if he was taken by surprise, insulted or confused. "Excuse me, sir?"

"Forget about it, son. We'll talk about it later. Have you been around this berg for any length of time?"

"Got in today, sir."

"Fair enough. Get on the main drag, head south. About two miles, you'll hit a roadhouse. Rosie's All-American. We're stopping there."

"Yes, sir."

They drove in silence until Bolan had the target spotted, coming at him on his left. It was your basic Western honkytonk, with mostly Jeeps and pickups parked out front. A pair of lonesome Harleys sat off to one side, in the shadows. He parked the Blazer, locked it up and followed Pike inside.

The nightclub's atmosphere reminded Bolan of the church in Laurin, after the two smoke bombs had exploded. Add a jukebox blaring nonstop country-western music from one corner, with a lot of tables fashioned out of giant wooden spools, some ancient-looking sawdust on the floor, and Rosie's could have passed for any cowboy bar between the Rockies and the coast. The barmaids wore fringed vests and leather miniskirts.

"Let's see...ah, here we go!"

Pike led him through the smoky room toward a booth against the southern wall. Two large, tough-looking men were there ahead of them, but Pike slid in beside the drinker on his left, waving Bolan toward the other empty seat.

"We saw the squad cars coming, Colonel," said the man on Pike's side of the booth. "I didn't think we ought to hang around."

"You did the right thing, Christopher," Pike replied.

"Who's this?" the man at Bolan's elbow asked suspiciously.

"A friend, I think. At least, he saved my ass back there."

"Oh, yeah?"

"Christopher Stone," Pike said nodding to the man beside him.

"Lou Doyle—" he motioned toward the man on Bolan's right "—meet Michael Belasko. From Wyoming, I believe."

"That's right, sir," Bolan said.

"Long way to come for church," Doyle commented.

"Well, I was in the neighborhood."

"Convenient, huh?"

"It was for me," Pike interrupted. "If you'd been there, Lou, you would have seen this man take down six of the enemy, including two armed officers."

"You helped a bit with one of those, sir," Bolan said.

"I try to keep my hand in," the colonel stated, braying laughter, flagging down the nearest waitress and ordering a pitcher for the table. When the beer was served and Pike had swallowed half the contents of his mug, he spoke again.

"They set us up, I'm telling you." His voice was bitter, but he didn't sound surprised. "Martz and the preacher make it out okay?"

"They're clean," Stone said. "There may be questions later on. I couldn't say."

"That's not a problem," Pike replied. "Preachers and politicians specialize in questions."

"I'll wait a bit," Stone said, "before I call to find out who's in custody."

"Don't be too obvious about it," Pike reminded him. "It's one thing if they're members, but we can't go bailing out the whole damn town."

"I'll handle it."

"What did you say your name was?" asked the man at Bolan's side.

"Belasko. Mike."

"You got ID?"

Pike glared across the table at him. "Lou, what's wrong with you?"

"I just don't like—"

"I *said* we'd check it out. Did you hear me say that?"

"Hey, all I'm sayin'—"

"All you're saying is that you don't trust my judgment. Is that right?"

That made Doyle hesitate. "No, sir," he said at last.

"I hope not, Lou. One thing I hate is insubordination."

"No, sir. What I mean—"

"We all know what you mean. It will be taken care of like I said, all right?"

"Yes, sir."

Bolan told himself he'd have to watch that one, then amended it. He'd have to watch all of them.

Damn right.

He forced a smile and sipped his beer.

3

Nine days before the brawl in Laurin, Bolan had been walking along the Mall in Washington, D.C., with Hal Brognola. "Catching rays," Brognola called it, but it hadn't been a social visit. They were talking business, and the game was deadly serious.

It was a strange day for it, with a tang of autumn in the air but clear skies overhead and sunshine beaming down. On every side were tourists checking out the nation's capital or civil servants on their lunch break. Off to Bolan's right stood the majestic National Gallery of Art; to his left was the equally imposing National Air and Space Museum. Pick a direction, and you could explore man's long quest in the heavens or his search for truth and beauty in the soul.

The truth that brought Bolan to Washington that afternoon would never be described by anyone as beautiful. He cherished beauty like the next man—maybe more so—but it had no lasting place in his life. He had been dwelling on the dark side for so long that it was hard for him to feel at home out of the shade.

"Nice day," Brognola commented, as they kept walking, with no reference to the briefcase he was carrying or the files inside.

"The best," Bolan agreed. Every day he woke up breathing was the best.

"Let's have a seat," the big Fed suggested, already veering toward an empty bench off to the left.

They sat. Another moment passed before Brognola said, "Are you familiar with the Paul Revere Militia?"

"Vaguely. I recognize the name, but that's about the size of it."

The whole militia movement had been making news for several years, even before the Oklahoma City bombing, back in 1995. According to the FBI's best data the various militia groups were independent of one another, though they sometimes kept in touch and mingled at the kind of "patriotic" rallies sponsored by the Ku Klux Klan and other racist, far-right groups. The membership appeared to be divided between professional haters—neo-Nazis, Klansmen, fire-breathing evangelists—and average people who had fallen on hard times. On the Great Plains, militia factions were a magnet for dispossessed farmers, bankrupt shopkeepers and the disciples of tiny, ultraconservative churches. Farther west they appealed to the same paranoia that had once fueled the Minutemen, the California Rangers and a dozen similar groups, attracting men and women who believed the Russians—or Chinese, Vietnamese, or whoever—had soldiers by the thousands hiding out in Mexico, prepared to charge across the border at a signal from the Kremlin...or the White House. Mostly they prepared to train and stockpile weapons for the day when they would have to fight and save America, but things had changed of late, out on the fringe.

The enemy these days was more often domestic in the grim scenarios these "patriots" devised. Instead of squaring off against the Russians or Red Chinese, they were preparing for a kind of Armageddon with the "Jewish world conspiracy" and all those liberals who still believed in medicare. With a conspiracy so vast, so deeply rooted in society, there were few allies the militiamen could trust.

Increasingly they fed on crackpot paranoia and prepared themselves for civil war.

And, some said, they were working overtime to start that war.

Brognola opened his attaché case and lifted out a fat buff-colored file. He laid the case aside and put the folder on his lap, one big hand weighting it, eyes flicking left and right around the Mall as if he thought someone would rush up to the bench and try to steal it from him.

"We have good reason to believe," he said at last, "that members of the Paul Revere Militia are engaged in acts of terrorism as an instrument of policy, perhaps approved—or plotted—by the leaders of the group. The bulk of these militias, as I'm sure you know, spend all their time collecting guns and canned goods, digging shelters, running silly-assed maneuvers on the weekends. Now and then some real nuts come along and soak up what they're selling, all that crap about the Jews on Wall Street, Commie gays in Washington, whatever, and you get something like Oklahoma City. Two or three weird bastards with a little training and a hard-on for the Feds, you never know."

"But you think this is different," Bolan prodded.

"Right," Brognola said. "It's overdue, if you stop and think about it. How long can these different groups exist, from coast to coast, before you get some kind of synthesis, collaboration, something? Think about that bunch that called themselves The Order, in the early 1980s. There were only twenty-five or thirty of them, but they came from everywhere—the Klan, Christian Identity, a couple different Nazi groups. They found a common cause, I mean to say. Before you knew it, they were robbing banks and printing funny money, bombing gay bars, drawing up hit lists— hell, they declared war on this country from a cabin out in Idaho somewhere."

"You're thinking instant replay?" Bolan asked.

"I'm thinking worse. The Order lasted only for about a

year. Their counterfeiting skills were so bad that they couldn't pass a bill without somebody getting busted. They were cocky from day one, and they got careless in a rush. Left tracks all over everything they did. For all the paramilitary rap, their personal security was shit. They were killing each other when the Bureau rolled them up in 1984.''

"Poetic justice," Bolan said.

"Except we can't count on a rerun. The Reveres are larger, better organized. They've been around since 1994, but it's the last twelve months or so they've really started getting militant. We have good reason to believe they've been involved in several acts of terrorism since last spring.''

"Informants?" Bolan asked.

"I'll get to that. Does Meyer Lowman's name ring any bells?''

"The DJ in Montana?"

"Very good. If you know that, you also know he was assassinated by persons unknown, a fairly professional drive-by, automatic weapons, the whole nine yards. That was in Billings. Next day, bright and early, comes a letter to the sheriff's office. No one thought enough of it to check for fingerprints until it was too late. The note says Lowman's number one, with more to follow. Enemies of the people will be called to account on the Day of the Blade.''

"Catchy title," Bolan said.

"It gets better. Wichita."

"The courthouse."

"Right again," Brognola said. "There was another letter, but the Bureau held it back. More shit about the Jews and how they run the world from New York or Miami Beach, I can't remember which. Down near the end, the letter says God's enemies should repent and prepare themselves for the Day of the Blade.''

Bolan waited this time, without comment, for his old friend to continue.

"Then, there was the Brinks truck at Ukiah. Three guards murdered in cold blood. The shooters walked away with close to four million. Untraceable. Next day…"

"Another note?"

"Bingo. Slick bastards sent it to a local newspaper this time. To make sure it went public, I suppose. Something along the line of how God's enemies are helping with their 'contributions' to prepare the way for his vengeance. Prepare for—you guessed it—the Day of the Blade."

"I'd say the novelty's worn off by now," Bolan said.

"Tell that to the Bureau," Brognola replied. "They've got a guy at Quantico who does nothing all day long but read and index far-out books and pamphlets from the fringe. I mean, that's all he does. This guy can look at sketches and describe the artist for you, what he looks like underneath his sheet. I don't know how he sleeps at night, with all that shit inside his head."

"The same way you do," the soldier stated.

"In that case, he has my sympathy. Whatever, someone has the brainstorm they should take the notes to Quantico and let this joker have a look. One peek, and he pulls out some old, self-published novel called *The Lancer Files*. You ever heard of it?"

"I'm way behind on leisure reading."

"From what I'm told, you haven't missed much. Basically it's one long rant against the Jews, the 'mud people,' the government in Washington, disguised as futuristic fiction. Some guy named Lancer is the hero and the title character. Long story short, the Jew-Red-homo-liberals take over Washington and make the U.S.A. one big slave-labor camp. This Lancer and a handful of his war-vet friends go underground and save the day—blow up the Congress and Supreme Court, this and that. The usual. My point is that they call their final blitz the Day of the Blade, for all the throats they're cutting. Clever, huh?''

"Somebody read the book, I take it.''

"Lots of people,'' the big Fed replied. "The publisher's been known to claim a million sales since 1989, but even if we knock three-quarters off for gross exaggeration, that's a lot of readers.''

"Still,'' said Bolan, "I don't see—''

"I'm getting there,'' Brognola interrupted him. "The author used a pen name, called himself Paul Freeman but we've checked the copyright. His real name is Ralph Pike, ex-colonel in the Special Forces, with a double tour in Vietnam. Two Silver Stars, a Bronze, three Purple Hearts.''

Brognola drew a glossy photo from the folder on his lap and handed it to Bolan. Two men seated in a car, at what appeared to be a drive-in restaurant, complete with carhops.

"That's Pike in the shotgun seat,'' Brognola said.

"So, what's he written lately?''

"Not much. He spends most of his time as national director of the Paul Revere Militia, since you ask.''

"Okay.''

"In fact he started the militia, back in 1994. Details are hazy, but we think he joined somebody else's group and hung out with them long enough to see that he could do a better job of it himself. Now, in the last twelve months, we've got a string of incidents in half a dozen western states that mirror various events from 'Freeman's' novel.''

"It's intriguing,'' Bolan said, "but inconclusive. Even granting he's a right-wing flake, that doesn't mean his people are the ones behind these crimes.''

"There's more,'' Brognola told him, and jabbed an index finger at the photo Bolan held. "The driver, there, is Christopher Stone, another one-time Green Beret. He was in Grenada. He was also on the ground in Panama before he pulled the pin and started working for the highest bidder.''

"Mercenary?''

"As they come," Brognola said. "Which kind of makes you wonder what he's doing with the Paul Reveres. They've got enough ex-military men already in the ranks, so they don't have to hire trainers. Even if they did, the paycheck wouldn't match what Stone took in last year alone, finessing weapons shipments to Saddam Hussein."

"He'll work for anybody, then."

"Anyone who pays top dollar, that would be. No half-assed, bargain-basement revolutionaries need apply."

"It's worth investigation," Bolan said.

"That's what the boys at ATF decided, but they had to play it cool. They're still in hot water from Waco, with the Branch Davidians, and that business with the Weaver family in Ruby Ridge."

"I thought that was the FBI."

"Bureau snipers did the shooting," Brognola replied, "but it was ATF that tried to hook him in the first place, catch him in a weapons sting and turn him as a mole inside one of those neo-Nazi outfits. Anyway, it didn't work."

"So, what was their approach with Pike?"

"One man, inside. Deep cover. He got close enough to make the brass think he was sniffing paydirt, maybe something they could hang indictments on. No details, but he gave them word of mouth, some names and faces. Working up to it, you know?"

"That kind of thing takes time," Bolan said.

"Right. But he ran out."

"What happened?"

"No one knows for sure," Brognola replied. "One night he missed a check-in with his partner, and that's it. Nobody's seen him since. There's been no word. It's like the guy was never there. Somebody cleaned out his apartment, clothes and all. Two possibilities—one is he may have turned."

"Or else, he's dead," Bolan said.

"Right. Smart money's riding on a shallow grave, but

no one has the first idea of where they should start looking."

"Sounds a little sloppy."

"It's not for me to judge," Brognola said. "Remember how the whole department took a beating back in 1988, with the Fort Smith sedition trial. We pulled in every major mouthpiece for the neo-Nazi fringe, eighteen of them, and piled on every charge that we could think of. Counterfeiting, weapons, racketeering, interstate conspiracy, receiving stolen property—the works."

"And everybody walked," Bolan said.

"Right." The bitterness was evident. "They laughed at us and walked."

"So no one's anxious for a replay unless they've got convictions guaranteed."

"At this point," the big Fed replied, "no one is interested in filing charges, period. The Bureau's begging off, afraid of more congressional investigations, and the ATF's already lost one agent, maybe two."

"How's that?" Bolan asked.

"One for sure," Brognola said. "The mole. And now his partner's pulled a fade. For all we know, Pike's shooters nailed them both."

"I don't see ATF ignoring two dead agents just like that."

"You assume they have a choice. I didn't mention that the Paul Reveres have friends in Washington."

Another photograph changed hands. This one portrayed a smiling man with one arm raised, a huge flag in the background, microphones in front of him.

"Neal Martz," Brognola said. "the freshman representative from Montana. He got himself elected on a promise to reduce the size of government at any cost, repeal the federal firearms laws and fight for an amendment to establish Christian prayer in public schools."

"He's with the Paul Reveres?" Bolan asked.

Brognola responded with a shrug. "I couldn't prove he ever paid the dues, but he's appeared with Pike at public functions more than half a dozen times, and we've got phone records that show the two of them reach out and touch each other two, three times a week. Of course, it could be social."

"Right."

"Or maybe not."

"Have you got more like him in Washington?"

"None so blatant," the big Fed replied, "but philosophically he's pretty close to mainstream for the GOP these days. I wonder sometimes whether it's a contract with America, or on America. The clowns these 'leaders' hang around with when they're sniffing after votes."

"Well, that's democracy."

"While it lasts." Brognola scowled and shook his head. "Don't get me started, okay? My point is, way back there when I had one, that there are guys like Martz in Congress who are second-guessing every move we make. Is it infringing on religious freedom if we bust some self-ordained messiah who's been making pipe bombs in his barn? Should we ignore a compound full of crazy people with machine guns if they stay on private property? J. Edgar must be spinning in his grave right now."

"So, what's the plan?" Bolan asked.

"That's the thing," Brognola answered, sounding hesitant. "The best plan I've been able to come up with is the one our friends at ATF already tried."

"Uh-huh."

"But with a twist, of course. You've got an edge."

"Which is?"

"You make the rules up as you go along. No need to build a case that stands alone in court."

Search and destroy, he meant to say, but still had trouble with the words, despite the countless times they had been down that road.

Bolan ignored that for a moment and said, "You mentioned a religious angle earlier. What's that about?"

Brognola took another glossy from the file and handed it across to his friend. It appeared to be a reproduction of a picture from some magazine with the caption cut away.

"Meet Reverend Alan Chalmers," Brognola said. "Up until the Paul Reveres were organized, he did his preaching from the Temple of All Souls, in Little Rock. Don't let the title fool you into thinking everyone was welcome, though. He's a Christian Reconstructionist, that one."

"I must have missed that day in Sunday school," Bolan commented.

"Everybody did if they were lucky. The Christian Reconstructionists believe that civil law and government are spawned by Satan and should be destroyed by any means available. The new laws, once they take control, will come straight out of the Old Testament. You know the rap—there's thirty, maybe forty capital offenses in the Book of Exodus alone. They rub you out for missing church or talking to a fortune-teller. Kids get snuffed for back talk to their parents. Gays? Forget about it."

"Pretty strict, in other words."

"Let's put it this way. Chalmers was among the first we know of to suggest that shooting an abortion doctor might just guarantee a trip to heaven for the triggerman. He's been connected with some clinic bombings, too. Served eighteen months in the late eighties for conspiracy on that. He wrote a book in jail."

"Like Hitler?"

"But without the humor," Brognola replied. "I've got a photocopy here if you want to treat yourself. One chapter's called 'God's Gift of AIDS.' The rest of it's a little morbid, though."

"And now he works with the militia."

"He's their chaplain," the big Fed told him. "Hell, why not? The guy's already proved his willingness to break 'man's law,' and he can reassure the troops that God's behind them all the way. Mix in the old identity refrain about how Jews are spawned from Satan and they did some kind of weird experiments in prehistoric times, producing 'mud people' like blacks and Asians, you've got a little something for everyone.''

"The kind of paranoia you're describing," Bolan said, "they won't be greeting everyone who wanders in with open arms."

"You'd need an angle, that's for sure."

"That's it? The plan?"

"I'm working on a cover...if you feel like doing this, I mean."

"Details," Bolan said, handing back the photographs.

"Ex-military man. You love America but hate the way she's going down the crapper. Queers and liberals, the no-win policy against our enemies, reverse discrimination that's been keeping you from any kind of decent job. The usual."

"I ought to have a record," the soldier stated.

"I'm way ahead of you. You did eight months in Mississippi for converting semiauto weapons for the Klan. The Bureau's got a dragon or a wizard on their payroll, some damn thing down there. He'll back your story if Pike's people check it out. The prison records will be fed in by computer, ditto on the military files."

"I sound a little paranoid," Bolan said.

"And pissed off. So, what do you think?"

"I'd like to read that file."

"It's your copy," the big Fed informed him, reaching back inside his briefcase for a paper bag to hold the sheaf of documents and photographs. "Just torch it when you're done."

"There's still that problem, making contact."

"The Reveres hold public meetings," Brognola said,

"advertised and everything. You'll find a schedule in there for the next two months or so."

"A meeting's not an introduction."

"I trust your instincts, but there's a possibility that I can help you out. When you've decided on a meeting, let me know the when and where. I'll see what I can do."

Bolan resisted asking what that meant. Some things were meant to take you by surprise.

"Okay," he said.

"Okay, you'll think about it, or okay, you'll do it."

"Let me read the file tonight. I'll go out west and have a look around, then let you know before I make connections."

"That's a deal," Brognola said. The grim expression on his face just might have been relief. "One thing about these guys."

"What's that?"

"They don't take prisoners."

"Who does?" the Executioner replied.

THAT EVENING, while leafing through the file in his motel room, Bolan had experienced a sense of déjà vu. He knew the kind of men who joined militias and affiliated groups, the vets and would-be heroes who had burned out on society, the changes they would never understand, much less accommodate.

In Bolan's mind it all went back to the Declaration of Independence. Written as a statement of principle, to justify the coming war with England some 220 years ago, that document had captured the essence of desperation in poetic terms:

When in the Course of human events, it becomes necessary for one people to dissolve the political bands which have connected them with another...

Who decided when a break was "necessary"? Was there any limit to the declaration's moral authority? In truth it had been causing trouble for the Union since the day it was written and ratified. Every group of American malcontents from Coxey's Army to the Black Panther Party had used Thomas Jefferson's rousing words as the justification for an armed assault against their chosen enemies—tax collectors, local cops, the White House. In the 1860s it had moved eleven states to form their own Confederacy and defend chattel slavery in a bloody civil war. And even once that cause was crushed by force of arms, the "principle" survived, enshrined in Washington and in the hearts of all Americans.

We hold these truths to be self-evident...

But if you don't quite see it our way, well, you have to go.

But when a long train of abuses and usurpations, pursuing invariably the same object, evinces a design to reduce them under absolute despotism, it is their right, it is their duty, to throw off such Government...

Whose right? Whose duty? Who defined "abuse" and "usurpation," much less "despotism"? One man's tyranny was another's Utopia. Those who complained most volubly about the breakdown in law and order were also those who seemed to hate their government the most and wish it gone.

The Executioner was heading west, toward long-familiar territory, but it wouldn't be the same this time.

One by one, he began to burn the pages of Brognola's file.

4

The Paul Revere Militia's rural headquarters was located in Bingham County, Idaho, to the southwest of Taber and Atomic City, near the county line. The nearest town of any size was Pocatello, forty miles to the southeast, but Colonel Pike's recruits took pride in severing their outward links to civilized society, which they regarded as corrupted and hopelessly enthralled to Communists and Jews—two labels they regarded as synonymous.

Brognola's file told Bolan that there had been no crimes definitely linked to the Reveres in Idaho. Of course, there were suspicions, from the bombing of a gay bar in Twin Falls to the unexplained disappearance of several Native Americans from the nearby Fort Hall Reservation and attempted sabotage at the U.S. Department of Energy's National Engineering Lab, in Butte County. But nothing could be proved, and no warrants were issued.

The compound sprawled over 150 wooded acres, the perimeter enclosed by barbed wire and patrolled by sentries around the clock. Living quarters were concentrated near the northeast corner of the property, a half mile from the unpaved road that granted access to the nearest county highway. In addition to a clapboard church and mess hall, an infirmary and several barnlike storage buildings, there were quarters for approximately sixty people, roughly two-thirds occupied. A hundred yards from the main complex, Pike and company had built their version of the FBI's Silhouette City to practice their marksmanship. False fronts of a dozen buildings featured gaping doors and windows where cutout figures would pop up at random, testing the shooter's ability to think and act under pressure. Overhead, suspended from a cable strung between two trees, a plywood mockup of a helicopter labeled ATF could be cranked back and forth to simulate a very limited and shaky aerial assault.

The drive south from Montana took them across the Continental Divide, past Liddy Hot Springs and Mud Lake, Bolan driving his Blazer in convoy with Pike's Jeep Cherokee. The mercenary, Stone, rode with him on the pretense of ensuring that he didn't lose his way. In fact their conversation took the form of an interrogation, subtle but well played, with the militia's second-in-command accumulating facts on Mike Belasko, filing them away for future reference.

Bolan didn't object. It was the game that he had come to play.

They reached the compound shortly after 1:00 a.m., with sentries stepping out to intercept them at the gate, saluting when they recognized the colonel. Bolan followed them inside and watched the gates swing shut behind him in his rearview mirror.

Infiltration wasn't the Executioner's specialty, per se, but he had played the game successfully on more than one occasion, dating back to his campaigns against the Mafia. The trick was being what your enemies expected you to be, but not so obvious that they suspected you on sight. The instant revolutionary who was too committed to a cause, the racist who was so extreme he walked in spouting genocidal nonsense off the street—such clumsy players would be swiftly tagged as either spies or lunatics, brushed off, perhaps eliminated for their trouble.

There was subtlety involved in penetration of a hostile camp. If he went overboard and seemed too eager, it could be as deadly as a phone call to Brognola on the colonel's private line. To strike a balance—that would be the key to life or death.

Stone directed Bolan to the quarters he would share with half a dozen men. Four were asleep when he arrived, the other two on guard duty. The building was constructed out of rough-hewn logs, with wooden shingles on the roof. A fire trap, if it came to that.

He filed the information and turned in.

NEXT MORNING he awoke to speakers blaring music that reminded Bolan of a German marching song from World War II. He couldn't place it, much less finger the composer, but he guessed the martial music would be part of Pike's routine to keep the troops in fighting trim.

With daylight breaking to the east, he had a better chance to check out the compound. There was a flagpole just outside the colonel's private quarters, but no sign of the stars and stripes as Bolan passed it and headed for the mess hall. Rather, Pike preferred a variation on the old colonial battle flag: a golden field behind the rattlesnake, prepared to strike across the words Don't Tread On Me.

The smallish mess hall was already filling up when Bolan got there. Everyone wore camouflage fatigues except him, making him stand out as a newcomer. There were men, women and children present, but the men predominated, roughly three to one. Suspicious eyes trailed Bolan from the mess-hall entrance to the serving line, until the colonel found him out of nowhere and stepped up to shake his hand.

"Sleep well?" Pike asked.

"Yes, sir."

"The mountain air. There's nothing like it. All that shit you have to breathe in town will kill you, mark my words."

"I wouldn't be surprised, sir."

"Right! Come on and eat, then, soldier."

They were serving porridge, powdered eggs, smoked bacon, toast and coffee, with milk for the kids. Bolan passed through the line with the same kind of stainless-steel tray he had carried at mealtimes in boot camp, trying not to be too obvious about the head count of those present or his scoping out the hall. Before the day was out, he meant to know as much about the property as possible.

He got another boost when Pike and Stone invited him to share their table. There was no sign of Lou Doyle, and Bolan didn't miss him, but he knew that he would have to watch out for the trooper who had shown immediate distrust of him the night before. It only took one carping voice, one pair of watchful eyes, to burn his cover down and get him killed.

Chris Stone had nearly finished eating by the time Bolan sat down, and he regaled the colonel with some tidbits from his chat with Bolan on the road. It sounded overly contrived to the Executioner's ears, and he was certain that the pair of them had covered this ground once already: his military record, his fictitious run-ins with the law.

"We don't hold prison time against a man," Pike said when Stone was finished. "It depends on what he did, of course. We don't want any baby-rapers, faggots or what have you. Still, there comes a time when real men, patriots, may have to take a stand against the tyranny of law imposed by aliens and traitors."

Bolan knew he was expected to reply and tried to keep it simple, unassuming. "Well, sir, I'll be honest with you. When those boys in Jackson hired me to convert their semi-autos, I was broke. I think I had about three dollars to my name, and the V.A. was jerking me around, as usual. The more I listened to them talk—the Klan, I mean—it seemed that some of what they said made sense. Not all of it. I mean, that stuff about the pope and all...I just don't know."

Pike waved a hand in front of him, as if he were fanning

flies. "Forget about that crap," he said. "Some of our Southern friends, for all of their sincerity, still think they're living in the 1920s. Hell, some of them think they won the Civil War!"

"Too bad they didn't," someone muttered at the far end of the table, off to Bolan's left.

"Our problem now," Pike said, ignoring the remark, "is that we've got a crew of so-called liberals in Washington and all across this country who have sold us out to communism and facilitated breakdown in the social order. Were you happy when the Russian bloc collapsed, Mike? Now, be honest."

Bolan shrugged. "I guess so, sure. Yes, sir."

"Damn right you were!" Pike said. "It was a freaking miracle. We won the cold war, for God's sake! But did you ever stop to ask yourself why it collapsed? That 'evil empire' Ronnie Reagan loved to talk about?"

"Well, the economy, I guess, sir."

"That's what Washington was hoping you'd believe," Pike said, eyes flashing as he made his point. "The truth is that the Soviet regime was scrapped because the Communists behind it didn't need it anymore. They had already captured Washington, their goal since 1917. What better way to lull the sheep stateside, than to demolish the Russian machine and rebuild their society into a mirror image of America? It didn't cost them anything, because they already had us. When they imitate American society in Russia, they're imitating their own creation!"

Bolan waited for the men around him to burst out laughing at some private joke, but the laughter didn't come. Except for Stone, who Bolan knew was in it for the money, all of them were clearly dedicated to Pike's paranoid view of recent history.

"I never thought about it that way, sir," he said at last.

"Of course not! You were raised to trust your leaders

and the media, like everybody else. You have to learn discrimination, soldier, just like any other fighting skill.''

''I see your point, sir.''

''We'll get you educated, son, don't worry. Educated, dedicated soldiers are the strongest in the world.''

''Yes, sir.''

The others stuck to small talk for a time, while Bolan cleaned his plate and rose to place it with the others left by those who finished ahead of him. When he was halfway there, somebody jostled him from his blind side, snarling, ''Watch your ass!''

He turned to face Lou Doyle, dressed in the camouflage fatigues that seemed to be the compound's standard uniform. Doyle stood with hands on hips, his mouth curled in a sneer.

''You got a problem, boy?'' he asked.

''Well, that depends,'' Bolan replied.

''Yeah? On what?''

''On whether you decide to bathe this year, or if they've got a gas mask in my size.''

''You need to worry more about a dental plan,'' Doyle said, ''after I kick your teeth in.''

''Make your move.''

His assailant feinted with a right, then fired a roundhouse left toward Bolan's head. It wasn't bad, but he was no Chuck Norris. The Executioner blocked the punch and stepped inside it, hammering a fist into Doyle's side, below his ribs.

The would-be soldier staggered, doubling over in his pain, and Bolan had a heartbeat to decide how he should finish it. The best way would be something lethal, to remove Doyle permanently from the scene, but that wouldn't endear him to the colonel or his live-in troops. Instead, he settled for a swift knee to the face, pulling the worst of it, rewarded with a satisfying crunch of cartilage as his adversary went down.

Ignoring Doyle as if he didn't see the body huddled at his feet, Bolan retrieved his tray and silverware, returned them to their proper place, and left the hall without a backward glance.

AN HOUR LATER he was watching half a dozen troopers work out with the silhouettes when Stone came looking for him. Bolan saw him coming but pretended not to notice.

"Doyle's okay," Stone said as he stepped up beside the Executioner.

"I'd have to disagree."

"I mean to say, you didn't kill him. Just in case you care."

"It wasn't preying on my mind."

Stone made a hissing sound that might have been a chuckle. "No," he said, "I didn't think so. Anyway, it's good you didn't kill him."

"Good for him."

"You, too. He's got some friends around the camp, as hard as you may find that to believe. They all know he's a smart-ass, and a couple of them saw him call you out for no good reason, but they might feel different if you stopped his clock.

"That isn't what I came for, anyway. The colonel wants to see you."

"Now?" Bolan asked.

"You got something else to do?"

He thought about that for a moment, finally shook his head and followed Stone across the compound to Pike's quarters. The mercenary rapped sharply on the door and waited.

"Come!"

Stone led the way and closed the door when Bolan was inside. The office had room for a military-surplus desk, three file cabinets and a folding table on the side, with a coffeemaker plugged into a wall outlet. The camp was powered by a generator housed behind the mess hall, insulated cables buried to prevent their cluttering the scenic view— or being cut by enemies.

"Please, have a seat," Pike said, directing Bolan to a folding chair that stood before the desk. He sat, aware of Stone behind him, as the colonel settled in his swivel chair.

"You did all right this morning in the mess hall," Pike went on.

"I didn't have much choice."

"We know that. Lou's been advised to watch his step. There's no accounting for the way some people click—or don't."

"No, sir."

"I made some inquiries this morning," the colonel said.

"Inquiries?"

"Don't be insulted, son, but we've had trouble with the government before. They've tried to infiltrate us several times, the state and federal boys alike. I had to check you out."

"I understand, sir."

"Anyway, I'm pleased to say you passed with flying colors. When I called your old friend down in the Magnolia State, he told me you were very helpful. Good with weapons, too, I understand."

"I try to keep my hand in, sir."

"That was a nasty business down at Parchman, though. The boy who tried to shank you."

Bolan blinked, pretending he was startled that the colonel had a way inside the penal system. "It was self-defense, sir."

"Of course," Pike said. "Shit happens. Now there's one less black dealing crack and raping white women. You should have been rewarded, but I understand they put you in the hole."

"For thirty days. Yes, sir."

"We're living in an age when self-defense is not politically correct," Pike said. "I'm sure you've grasped that fact by now. The welfare state demands that we sit back and let ourselves be robbed, raped, butchered in the name of understanding. I was watching CNN the other day, some crap about a baby-sitter from Honduras—an illegal alien, of course—who's been molesting children in Miami. Her defense attorney's claiming that Latino culture raises women with the need to fondle naked children. It's a big misunderstanding, see? Your liberals are up in arms about the setback to their multicultural agenda. God preserve us."

"Yes, sir."

"Anyway, I'm getting off the track," Pike said, and smiled. "My point is that you're clean, as far as I'm concerned, and you have talents we could use in the militia if you're interested. If you need time to think about it—"

"No, sir," Bolan said. He didn't want to overdo it, trying for the right blend of emotions—gratitude, with some resentment—as he said, "There's nowhere else for me to go."

Pike studied his face again for a moment before he said, "There is a matter of initiation. We don't take it lightly, son."

"No quitters," Stone stated from behind him, with a cold edge to his voice.

"You're no threat to us now if you decide to walk away," Pike told him. "We've shared a meal, you spent the night—so what? But if you stay, there may be things you see and hear that could be useful to our enemies. We can't sit still for leaks."

"I handle the security myself," Stone said to emphasize the threat. "I take it very seriously."

"So would I," Bolan replied.

"Well, then, so we understand each other." Pike was smiling as he rose, behind his desk. "If you'll stand up..."

Bolan stood.

"Are you a Christian, son?"

"I never really thought about it, sir."

"We'll work on that, and skip the Bible for the moment. Raise your right hand and repeat the oath with me."

Bolan stood waiting, eyes locked with the colonel's, hoping he could match the older man's apparent zeal. Behind him he could almost feel Stone watching, hard eyes boring into him like pistol barrels jammed between his shoulder blades.

No turning back, but what the hell? A vow made to the very enemies whom he intended to destroy meant less than nothing. It was like a promise scratched in desert sand before a driving wind.

"I," Pike said, "insert your name—"

"I, Mike Belasko..."

"Swear upon my life and honor to uphold the principles and standards of the Paul Revere Militia—"

He solemnly repeated it, with no time to think twice about the sour taste those words left in his mouth.

"And to do everything within my power as a soldier of the Paul Revere Militia to defend the U.S. Constitution as originally written."

Interesting, Bolan thought. That erased the last sixteen amendments, everything from income tax and women's suffrage to presidential term limits and civil rights for blacks.

"I understand my duty," Pike went on, "to serve the cause of liberty with every fiber of my being, every breath and with the last drop of my blood. I promise solemnly to die before I will disclose the secrets of the Paul Revere Militia to the enemies of freedom, whether dwelling in this nation or abroad."

He managed not to choke on the idea of promising to die for men he meant to take down.

"In the event that I betray this trust, whether deliberately or through some act of negligence, I willingly submit myself to discipline from the commanders and my fellow soldiers in the Paul Revere Militia."

Bolan mouthed the lie without a hitch.

"So help me, God."

"So help me, God," he said, and let his hand drop to his side.

Stone clapped him on the back and stepped around in front of Bolan, while the colonel came to shake his hand. They both seemed genuinely pleased to have him—or the man they thought he was—as one more member of their private army.

"Welcome to the Paul Reveres," Pike said. "You'll do us proud, I have no doubt."

"I hope so, sir."

"You'll have to undergo some training first, of course," Stone told him.

"Consider it as a refresher course," the colonel offered. "We're in constant training here, no one exempted. I still run the course and qualify with weapons twice a month, like everybody else. You'll do just fine."

To which the Executioner replied, "When do I start?"

5

They started after lunch, another mess-hall gathering, another serving line. It came as no surprise to Bolan when Pike and Stone ignored him. He was in the army now and starting at the bottom. There were no more cozy breakfasts with the brass in Bolan's future, unless he did something worthy of acclaim.

But he would deal with first things first.

The camouflage fatigues he wore were new and fit him well enough. Pike's private army seemed to have a ready source of army-surplus gear available, from furniture and clothing to the lethal hardware he had seen the sentries packing on their beats. Most citizens' militias got along with motley arsenals donated by their members, anything from lever-action Winchesters to more-sophisticated sporting versions of standard military rifles, but the Paul Reveres seemed better equipped, from what he could see. The guards were armed with Colt AR-15s, the preban models that included muzzle breaks, extended magazines and bayonet lugs, some of them the shorter carbines with collapsing stocks. Those men with side arms—roughly two-thirds of those Bolan had observed—all carried semiautomatic pistols in 9 mm or .45-caliber, to reduce the inventory of mixed ammunition on hand. The tower guards, posted at half a dozen points around the camp, were armed with Heckler & Koch sniper rifles, complete with telescopic sights.

Whatever Pike and Stone were up to, they would never be accused of working with substandard matériel...except, perhaps, where human beings were concerned.

Lou Doyle was several minutes late to noonday mess. Bolan had found a place with half a dozen strangers at the northeast corner of the hall, and they had finished off their introductions by the time Doyle entered, sporting two black eyes and white adhesive tape across a broken nose.

"You'll have to watch yourself with Lou," said one of Bolan's new acquaintances, a sandy blonde named Rick Guarini.

"Oh? Why's that?" Bolan asked.

"I don't think he likes you," Jesse Rafferty suggested, chuckling to himself.

"Too bad we didn't hit it off."

"You hit it off, all right," Guarini said. "You snapped his fuckin' beak, is what you did."

"His problem," Bolan said.

"Just watch your back, is all I'm sayin'. Word to the wise, okay?"

"I hear you."

"Fair enough."

When lunch was done, the compound's speakers blared a call for soldiers to assemble on what passed for a parade ground, in the center of the camp. Bolan fell into line beside Guarini, fourth row from the front, and spotted Doyle glancing back at him, across one shoulder. Bolan half expected him to curse or even make a move.

Instead, he smiled.

It was unsettling, but Bolan shrugged it off. Some kind of exercise was shaping up, and it would be his first test with the Paul Reveres. He had no fear of falling short, but it would be a challenge to excel in such a way that Pike and Stone would notice him, consider adding Bolan to their list of active terrorists instead of relegating him to useless garrison duty.

They had been standing in the sun for several minutes when the colonel joined them, Stone close on his heels. Pike's number two was carrying a submachine gun slung across his shoulder. Bolan recognized it as an H&K MP-5S D-3, the model with a telescoping butt and heavy-duty sound suppressor installed before it left the factory.

"We've got a little exercise lined up for you this afternoon," Pike told his troops. "You'll be divided into six-man teams, each with a separate color designation—red, blue, green and gold. You'll each draw weapons—" as he spoke, Stone raised his submachine gun overhead "—and three spare magazines. We're using blanks today, paint rounds, but you'll observe the standard weapons protocol. Remember, even blanks can kill you if you don't know what you're doing."

Pike let that sink in for a bit before continuing. "When you've been armed and drawn your colors," he continued, "you'll be sent in various directions, given twenty minutes' marching time before the exercise begins. No maps, but each team will have one man with a compass. Once the exercise begins, you'll have three hours on the clock to stalk and kill as many of the other three teams as you can. And people, they'll be stalking you."

He paused again before asking, "Do I hear any questions?" No one spoke or raised a hand, and Pike seemed satisfied. "All right," he said at last, "fall out on my command and draw your gear. Fall out!"

Stone met them at the compound's armory, where colored badges, weapons and spare magazines of harmless ammunition were dispensed. He called off names before they started drawing gear, and Bolan wound up on the green team, with Rafferty and Guarini. Lou Doyle drew red and started making noise about commanding his team in the field. No one among his teammates bothered to dispute him, and the broken-nosed commando hardly spared a glance at Bolan as he drew his gear.

The compound had enough MP-5 SD-3s to go around, and Bolan checked his magazines to verify that they were loaded with the special splatter rounds that would mark kills for subsequent determination by a referee. It had been years since he'd participated in a war game without lethal intent, but it required the same skills Bolan used in each campaign against his real-world enemies. The only difference this time would be that a trigger pull spilled poster paint instead of blood.

Guarini was the senior member of their team, with eighteen months in the militia, and since all of them were privates, he assumed command with no dissenting voices from the ranks. It made no difference to the Executioner who led them on the exercise, as long as he found opportunities to score against their adversaries in a major way.

When everyone was armed and outfitted, Stone passed among them, designating a different point of the compass for each team—north, south, east and west. Their basic orders were to hike straight out for twenty minutes, then select a target and direction of their choice and go for broke. All casualties would sling their weapons and return to camp, without exception. Time would be called at 4:30 p.m., unless one team had cleared the field before that time, and each team would be graded on the basis of its kills. Survivors from the winning team—or teams, in the event they came up with a tie—would be excused from one day's normal duty in the camp as a reward.

Guarini's green team was directed to the south and wasted no time jogging out of camp. Five minutes later they had left the settlement behind, slowing the pace a bit as they marched through a forest of juniper and ponderosa pine, alder and quaking aspen. Ferns and thistles brushed their legs in passing, making muffled whisper sounds.

"That's time," Guarini said when they had marched for twenty minutes. "The way it looks, we've got the gold

team to our west, the red team to our east—your old friend
Lou,'' he said to Bolan, with a crooked grin.

''Your call,'' Rafferty said.

''It's downhill to the east, but there's all kinds of gullies
from the runoff. It'll slow us down, and we'll be making
too much noise to sneak up on a deaf man. West it is.''

It took them half an hour to find the first trace of their
quarry. Bolan spotted it, a deep gouge in the loam where
someone had begun to lose his footing on the slope and
dug in with his boots to stop the slide. A sapling had been
broken, too, most likely when the soldier grabbed it to preserve his balance. Bolan checked the oozing sap and found
it moist, still nearly fresh.

''Okay, heads up,'' Guarini whispered. ''Keep in mind,
this is supposed to be like the real thing. No fun and
games.''

They fanned out in a skirmish line and started ghosting
through the trees, each man alert to fallen twigs and leaves
before he put his foot down, minimizing noise, alert to any
sight or sound of their intended prey. Bolan was in the
zone, prepared to make the game seem real—like life and
death—for anyone who crossed his path.

A voice up ahead alerted them to contact. Someone had
stumbled and had cursed in reflex action, catching it too
late. Another voice hissed at the first man to be quiet,
thereby adding to the noise, as Bolan closed in on his mark.
He felt the others, off to either side of him, and had no
way of telling what was going through their minds or how
their nerves were jangling at that moment. How many of
them had honest military training, versus games like this?
How many had been called upon, in combat or civilian life,
to kill another human being?

Bolan wondered whether some of those on his own team
might be responsible for any of the crimes detailed in Hal
Brognola's file. He didn't want to think so, but he also
knew that sympathy, the roots of friendship, couldn't be

allowed to tamper with the purpose of his mission. When the time came, he would act on instinct, with grim determination and all the martial skill at his disposal.

But for now, this moment, it was still a game.

He spotted movement up ahead, glanced left and right to check for more of the enemy. With six men on a team, that left two-thirds of the gold force still unaccounted for. Strict logic told him that they had to be nearby, but where? Suppose the noisy pair was bait, instructed to reveal themselves and draw in careless hunters to a killing stand?

There had been no time for his adversaries to build traps, and they could only mark a kill with paint-round hits, in any case. The danger would be in an ambush, then, and so far Bolan saw no sign of anybody lurking in the shadows or the branches overhead. It would be difficult to climb the lofty pines without some special gear, and any gunners well above the forest floor would find their fields of fire obstructed by the boughs beneath them.

Clear, then, for the moment.

"Will you hurry up, for Christ's sake!"

"I'm coming, dammit!"

Voices were clearly audible, and nothing suggested that they were playing. Stragglers? It was very possible in this terrain. If one or two had lagged behind a bit and gotten separated from their team, they would be anxious to catch up and score some kills, not thinking of themselves as targets.

Bolan had the fire selector on his weapon set for 3-round bursts as he closed in, remembering that paint rounds wouldn't have the recoil of normal 9 mm ammunition. It was possible to overcompensate and miss your target that way, just as surely as if you allowed the piece to buck and get away from you.

He was ahead of Rick Guarini and the others as he closed the gap to thirty feet. At that range he was sure the two men from the gold team were alone, no backup waiting in the shadows. Bolan whistled softly and watched them turn before he stroked the trigger on his SMG. Once, twice, the paint rounds splattered on impact, smearing chests, necks and faces while the startled men stood and gaped at him in dumb surprise.

"Hey, where did—?"

"You're dead," Guarini told them, coming through the trees a heartbeat later. "Dead men don't be talking. Head on back to camp."

When they were gone, Guarini turned to Bolan with a small frown on his face. "You're pretty good," he said. "You done this kind of thing before, I take it."

"Something like. We've got four to go."

"Okay," Guarini said, "let's roll those bad dogs up!"

They moved off through the woods again, following signs now, tracking their prey by footprints, scuff marks, the still-damp stain where one of their targets had stopped to urinate against a tree trunk. Within ten minutes, moving quietly, they had drawn close enough to see the last man in the line, plodding along a narrow game trail through the forest.

At a signal from Guarini, they fanned out on both sides of the trail, no order spoken, leaving Bolan free to move ahead and let the others catch up as they could. Guarini didn't protest, maybe sensing that he had a first-rate killer on his team who would ensure a decent score.

Before he closed to killing range with the straggler, Bolan had already spotted the rest of the team. They were strung out along the trail, some twenty feet apart. It was careless of them not to notice two men missing from the group, but that was their problem, not his. The trick now was to take them down as rapidly as possible, before they had a chance to rally and respond. In this game, unlike combat, any hit by paint rounds was considered fatal—or at least debilitating—and the wounded man was out of play. That made kills easier for skillful shooters, but it also meant that any lucky shot—a graze, whatever—would take Bolan out, as well. And he needed victory to advance his cause with the militia brass.

Which led him to decide that he should charge.

It would be safer to snipe from the trees, but he couldn't be sure of nailing all four men before at least a couple of them went to ground, returning fire. And once his adversaries started shooting back, anything could happen. Even if he didn't wind up splashed with paint, the other members of his team would be at risk.

When less than thirty feet of open ground lay in between his straggling target and himself, the Executioner stepped out of cover, rushing forward while squeezing off a silenced 3-round burst that struck his adversary from behind and plastered down his hair with yellow paint. Still charging, Bolan roughly shoved the "dead" man to one side, off balance, where he sprawled in the underbrush before he could return fire, accidentally or otherwise.

A strangled cry of warning from the man alerted his companions even as he fell, and Bolan saw them turning as he made his charge, the MP-5 SD-3 raised to shoulder height and steady in a firm two-handed grip. He thumbed the fire selector switch to full-auto, hosing them with half a magazine before the startled soldiers knew exactly what was happening. His paint-filled slugs made little smacking sounds on impact, blossoming on flesh and fabric, making one guy blink and curse as paint got in his eye.

"Hey, where the hell did *you* come from?"

"We tracked you down," Guarini said, coming up on Bolan's flank in time to witness the exchange. "No back talk from the dead folks now, you hear?"

"You sneaky bastards!"

"I suppose if it was on the other foot, you would of called us for a stand-up fight?" When no one answered him, Guarini said, "I didn't think so. Y'all head back to camp, and don't forget to check in with the ref."

"Goddamn!"

They heard the men muttering as they retreated toward the compound, giving up on any effort to make silent progress through the trees.

"You *have* done this before," Guarini commented.

"Enough to know one thing."

"Oh? What's that?"

"If anybody had the same idea we had, to hunt another team, they'll hear that noise and zero in."

"You think?"

"It's what I'd do," Bolan replied.

"You reckon we should follow them awhile?"

"It couldn't hurt. And if no one takes the bait, we've still got time to double back, try something else."

"Sounds good. Let's do it."

Bolan took the point, without requesting it or waiting for an order from Guarini. By now there was no doubt in Guarini's mind who had the savvy to command, and he appeared relieved that Belasko didn't challenge him, instead consulting, friendly like, and making the decisions sound as if they were Guarini's idea when he announced them to the team at large. Guarini let the new boy rove ahead without complaint, convinced that he would stand a better chance of finding targets than any other member of the team.

Bolan trailed the gold team at a distance, letting them fade out of view as he brought up the rear. He had no hope of overtaking them, to intercept an ambush party waiting anywhere between them and the camp, so he would have to count on someone tracking from the flank and try to turn the hunters into prey.

If they existed.

There was at least a fifty-fifty chance that members of the blue team would have headed in the opposite direction, stalking Lou Doyle's reds, off to the east. In that case there would be no one between the gold team and the compound. Bolan would be wasting time...but that was part of hunting, whether you were out for rabbits, deer or men. You had to take your chances, go through all the motions. The end result, in many cases, owed as much to luck as to the hunter's skill.

He froze as subtle movement on his left alerted him to something creeping through the trees. It seemed unlikely that a deer or other animal of any size would linger in the neighborhood after the gold team wandered past, exuding noise and wounded pride, but anything was possible. He watched and waited, saw the shadow-shape take human form and edge into an errant ray of sunlight.

Bolan couldn't name the soldier, but the red badge clipped to the lapel of his fatigue shirt marked him as a member of Doyle's team. He had to have traveled hard to get this far in the amount of time that had elapsed, and traveled quietly, as well. He had the gold team spotted, and the only question now was whether he could read their body language, guess from all the racket they were making that they had been taken out of play. If so, there would be no point in pursuing them. And yet...

The man was framed in Bolan's sights, but he was hesitant to fire. Where were the others from his team? It made no sense that he would come this far alone.

Something hissed past Bolan's face and struck the tree beside him. The soldier ducked away, half expecting to be sprayed with paint, but splinters stung his flesh instead. A second round gouged bark out of the tree trunk, while the third clipped off a fern to Bolan's left.

Live rounds!

The game had taken a bizarre and deadly turn. Someone had switched the paint rounds in his weapon for a standard killing load, and while he couldn't see the shooter yet, his first suspect was Lou Doyle. If he was wrong on that score, if there was a madman in the camp, for instance, and his choice of marks was random, Doyle might well be innocent, but the coincidence was too extreme for Bolan's liking.

Moving fast, he ducked behind an oak in time to hear

more bullets strike the tree, the shots behind them barely audible, a whisper like the sound an airgun makes, some distance off. The submachine gun in his hands was worthless now, unless he had a chance to use it as a club or blind his unseen adversary with a paint round to the eyes. He slung the piece across his back to free his hands, and reached down to his boot, where his Bearpaw knife nestled in a spring-clip leather sheath.

It was the next-worst thing to being empty-handed, when his adversary had an automatic weapon and at least some skill in using it, but Bolan wasted no time mourning the poor hand he had been dealt. If he could only spot his enemy, then close the gap between them to a point where he could throw the knife—or, better yet, reach out and touch someone—he had at least a fighting chance.

He had to move, draw fire and hope that he could spot his adversary in the process. Sitting still would only give his enemy a chance to move in for the kill, outflank him, pin him down.

He broke from cover to his right and lunged in the direction of a nearby fallen tree, eyes sweeping in the general direction that the early rounds had come from. There! Was that a man-shape in between those pines, or were the shadows playing tricks on him?

The bright wink of a muzzle-flash was followed instantly by sounds of angry hornets sizzling through the air. He reached the fallen tree, dived headlong into cover, knowing he had found his man.

Still, reaching him would be another game entirely—a laborious procedure, highly dangerous, perhaps impossible. It meant that he would have to keep on circling, try to close the gap without getting killed in the process, while his enemy was on alert and watching for him, ready with an SMG against his five-inch blade.

Not hopeless, maybe, but close.

He was about to try a new approach, crawl for a while instead of standing up and charging through the trees, when

Rick Guarini and the other members of his team caught up with him. They didn't see him, didn't seem to notice anything, in fact, proceeding toward the hidden gunner at a steady, stalking pace.

"Watch out!" Bolan shouted, hoping he could warn them off in time. "We've got live rounds in play!"

"Say what?"

The words had barely passed Guarini's lips before the hidden submachine gun stuttered one more time, and the team leader went down, arms flailing as he fell, a splash of crimson on his shirtfront that was anything but poster paint.

The other members of the green team went to ground, one of them cursing. Somewhere off to Bolan's left, he heard a crashing in the undergrowth, receding swiftly, as his would-be killer broke and ran. Too many witnesses, perhaps, or maybe he was satisfied with his achievement. Either way it would be suicide to chase him through the woods, armed only with a knife, not even knowing if he was alone.

He went to check Guarini, staying low in case there was another sniper waiting in the shadows, but no more live rounds were fired in their direction. Guarini had taken one round in the shoulder, but there was no apparent damage to the joint or nearby vital organs. He was cursing steadily when Bolan reached him, vowing payback on the stupid bastard who had nearly killed him, playing cowboy.

"Who was that?" another member of the team asked.

"Some crazy bastard," came an answer from the ranks.

"If I find out who it was, I'm gonna kick his ass," a third man said. "At least."

"Before you do that," Bolan said, "you need to watch your own. We've got a long walk back to camp, and someone out there doesn't seem to like us very much."

6

The colonel was angry when told of the incident, but there was little he could do, in concrete terms, about the ambush in the woods. Chris Stone was logging in the gold-team members, "killed" in action, when the members of the green team came in, carrying their wounded leader, and he summoned Pike, along with the med-school dropout who served as the militia's live-in medic. Four men from the paint-smeared gold team carried Guarini to the infirmary, Stone leading, while Pike faced the other greens.

"What happened out there?" Pike demanded.

"Someone started firing live rounds," Bolan replied. "Guarini took one in the shoulder, and whoever popped him made a run for it."

"You heard the shots?" Pike asked.

"No, sir. The shooter worked with a suppressor."

"Did it seem like he was going for Guarini?"

Bolan hedged. "It's hard to say, sir. I was on the point. First thing I know, we've got incoming rounds, but they're not paint balls. Rick walked into it before I had a chance to warn the squad."

"Did you see anything?"

A flat-out lie to that one. He wasn't prepared to finger Doyle's red team. Not yet.

"There may have been a shadow, sir. Again it's hard to say. Once I decided they were live rounds coming in, I didn't have much chance to scope the source."

Pike raised one fist, chest high, and clenched it so tight that his knuckles popped. An angry flush had brought color to his face, as he stood ramrod straight before them, cobalt eyes regarding each of them in turn from under bristling brows.

"I'm not about to let this go," he said. "Don't think I am. Turn in your arms to Captain Stone right now, and go back to your quarters. I'll be calling in the others, and we'll find out who the hell's responsible for this."

The members of the green team did as they were told. Five minutes later the loudspeakers in the compound blared a trumpet call that echoed far and wide through the surrounding woods. A summoning. It took the better part of half an hour for the unscathed red and blue teams to return, approaching from near-opposite directions. Bolan watched Doyle's reds march past, picking out the profile of the soldier he had glimpsed before the shooting started. Doyle passed by without a sidelong glance, ignoring Bolan, if he even noticed he was being watched.

There was an inquiry of sorts: Chris Stone examined all the weapons and spare magazines, determining that none of them was loaded with live rounds. The verdict came as no surprise to Bolan. He had counted on the shooter ditching any evidence that might incriminate him, on the long hike back to camp. Shell casings probably remained around the ambush site, but it would take ballistics experts to compare them with at least two dozen submachine guns in the camp, check out extractor marks and the impressions made by firing pins. Even then, the answer would be up for grabs, since guns had been distributed before the game without the recipients signing for specific weapons, recording their serial numbers. By the time the test got that far, any fingerprints would have been smudged or wiped away.

Forget it.

He assumed the shooter would have stashed his magazine of live rounds somewhere in the woods, but they could search forever without finding anything. Stone questioned everyone who had participated in the game, beginning with the reds and blues, but no one else had seen the shooter or admitted any knowledge of his handiwork. They didn't have a polygraph in camp, and everyone Stone grilled seemed so sincere that by the time he finished, Stone himself was leaning toward the notion of a gunman from outside the compound.

"Think about it," he told Pike, with Bolan standing by. "What better way for someone from the Bureau or the ATF to set us at one another's throats? It's classic. Think of all the underhanded shit they used to pull against the Klan, way back."

"It's possible," Pike answered, waiting to be sold on the idea. He turned to Bolan, saying, "Still, you had that beef with Lou this morning, over breakfast."

Bolan shrugged. "If I knew it was him, I'd tell you, sir. He may be pissed at me—I'd bet on it, in fact—but I can't say he did the shooting."

"Well, that's honest, anyway," Pike said. "If I find out it *was* Lou Doyle, I promise you, I'll have his balls for cuff links. As it is, though…"

"Yes, sir. Understood."

"I'll have something to say at mess this evening. You're on watch, Belasko, if you still feel up to it."

"No problem, sir."

"Good man. Dismissed."

He stopped by the infirmary to check on Rick Guarini. They couldn't report a gunshot wound without inviting scrutiny from the police, which would inevitably lead to questions, an inspection of the weapons they were using in their exercise—no end, in short, of trouble for the Paul Reveres. It was the same mind-set he had observed in various guerrilla bands around the world. If noncombatant members of the family got sick, beyond the expertise of medics living with the group, they would accept aid when and where it was available. As for the soldiers, though, they understood the risks involved when they signed on, and for the most part didn't grumble when their lives were on the line.

Guarini wasn't dying, as it happened. He was stoned on morphine—stolen from a Boise medical supplier, Bolan later learned—but he had come through the extraction of the bullet in good shape and was expected to recover fully once he got some rest. Right now his bloodshot eyes were dreamy looking, and he had a tendency to grin when nothing funny had been said.

"They know who shot me, man?" he asked.

"Not yet. We're working on it."

"Save a piece for me when you find out who it was," Guarini said.

"Sounds like a plan. Right now you need to get some rest, though, so you have the strength to deal with him."

"I'll fuckin' deal with him, don't worry." He grinned even as he tried to sound belligerent. "Damn clumsy bastard, switching rounds like that. What kind of idiot...?"

His voice trailed off, and Bolan left him nodding. Clearly, in his weakened state, no one had raised the possibility of a deliberate shooting. Guarini assumed it had been accidental, someone's negligence, and that the guy who blew it would confess his error—maybe take a beating or some other form of rough-and-ready punishment—to make things right.

The colonel and Chris Stone thought otherwise, knew that the incident was calculated, but their paranoia—Pike's, at any rate—led them to look outside the group for triggermen. The world was full of enemies who hated the militia: gays and feminists, environmentalists and welfare mothers, federal agents, grafting politicians, various minorities—the list went on forever. How crazy was it to assume that one or two of those determined adversaries might decide to score a coup by striking at the very heart of operations for the cause?

He couldn't rule it out, by any means, and yet...

It didn't seem to Bolan that the Feds would operate that way, regardless of his own instructions and clandestine mission. He had been recruited, with the team at Stony Man, specifically because the government in Washington didn't have the resolve or willing personnel to carry out those operations where the Constitution was suspended, civil rights went out the window and the so-called simple answers were pursued at any cost. An isolated lawman here and there was prone to gun down his suspects ahead of going to trial, no doubt, and there were SWAT teams, Delta Force, the Navy SEALs—whatever—to contend with hostage situations and the like, but no one was prepared or authorized to kill for killing's sake on native soil.

No one, that is, but Bolan and a handful of associates who worked for Hal Brognola.

A team of federal agents might have tried to infiltrate the compound, one of them firing on instinct when he met armed adversaries in the forest. Covering their bureaucratic asses would be second nature in a case like that, and while it had the ring of plausibility, his gut still told him he was looking at an inside job.

Which brought him back to Doyle.

It could be anyone, of course, but the selection of Bolan as the target, not long after he'd humiliated Doyle in front of witnesses, filled out the classic homicide detective's checklist: motive, means and opportunity. Until such time as Doyle was positively cleared or someone else was fingered as the shooter's target—an unlikely prospect in itself—Bolan would watch his back and keep an eye out for the broken-nosed commando everywhere he went.

Guarini's shooting was the topic of discussion over supper in the mess hall. Bolan sat with other members of his green team, plus a couple from the gold squad, who ex-

pressed their grudging admiration for his kills that afternoon, proceeding quickly to the questions that were foremost on their minds. Had he glimpsed anything? Who was
the shooter really trying to eliminate? Was it a crazy accident, or what? He had no answers, leaving them disappointed as he cleaned his tray and went to check in with
the sergeant of the guard.

Before he left the mess hall, Bolan spotted Doyle and
made a point of walking past his table, made a point of
checking out the soldier sitting next to him. He knew the
face—the profile, anyway—from their encounter in the
woods, before the bullets started flying. On the left breast
of his camo shirt, a cloth ID tag gave his name as
Cartwright.

Fair enough.

The sergeant of the guard was fifty-something, five foot
seven, with the stocky build and shaved head of a wrestler.
He was chewing a cigar but didn't light it, making Bolan
wonder if he devised some kind of compromise with cancer
in his mind.

"You're on perimeter tonight," the sergeant said, "assuming you're okay with that."

"No problem."

"'Cause I heard you had some trouble on the exercise
this afternoon."

"Not me," the Executioner replied.

"One of your friends got shot, is what I hear." The
sergeant forged ahead, as if he hadn't spoken. "Thing like
that, sometimes it takes the edge off, if you get my drift."

"My edge is right where it's supposed to be."

The sergeant smiled. "That's what I like to hear."

He fetched a Colt Commando from the armory, the
shorter version of the M-16 A-1, initially designed to serve
the function of a submachine gun with a rifle's stopping
power. Other than the shortened barrel and the telescoping
butt, it was identical to standard-issue rifles of the U.S.

military, sling and all. The web belt Bolan strapped around his waist supported a canteen, a flashlight, walkie-talkie and an ammo pouch with three spare magazines inside. The first thing the Executioner did was to check to make sure they were loaded, live rounds all the way. Short of unloading all four magazines and shaking every round, he couldn't guarantee the cartridges were good, but neither could he think of any reason why the sergeant—or the colonel, for that matter—should desire to see him killed.

Three other sentries showed up in the next five minutes, drawing gear identical to Bolan's. Two of them were wearing belt knives—one Ka-bar and one trench knife, a brass-knuckled knockoff of the World War I original—which made him conscious of the slim stiletto tucked inside his boot. At close range it would do the job as well as larger blades, assuming Bolan let his adversary bring the action hand to hand.

Assuming he would have a choice.

"Okay, let's go," the sergeant said. They trailed him to an open military-style jeep and climbed in, while the sergeant slid behind the wheel. "I'll drop you on your beats and bring out your relief at midnight. In the meantime stay awake, look sharp and don't forget we had a prowler on the grounds this afternoon. You spot something, don't be afraid to use your rifles or your radios."

The woodland road was narrow, badly rutted, overhung with limbs that nearly grazed the jeep, while ferns and bushes scraped its sides. Ten minutes out the sergeant braked and turned to Bolan.

"Here you go," he said, and pointed into darkness off to Bolan's right. "The fence is that direction, ten or fifteen yards. You're in the middle of your beat right now. Five hundred yards in each direction, back and forth. Stay on the wire, and you can't go wrong. Okay?"

"Okay."

"Don't break a leg," the sergeant cautioned, grinning as he put the vehicle in gear. "We'd have to shoot you."

Bolan waited for the jeep's taillights to fade, then killed another moment standing in the darkness, while his night eyes made their gradual adjustment. He would save the flashlight for a dire emergency, perhaps the broken leg he had been warned about, and trust his combat skills as far as possible.

No sweat, he told himself. He was on patrol, a normal shift like everybody else.

But with a difference, right.

The man or men who had already tried to kill him once would have no difficulty finding out where Bolan was. Ten minutes' driving time would make a fair hike from the central camp, but he—or they—could take it overland, instead of sticking to the ring road and reduce the travel time that way. Some stealth would be required on the approach, but every member of the Paul Revere Militia in the compound had been trained right here, in these same woods. They would have pulled guard duty, some of them where Bolan stood right now, and it would be familiar ground, providing an important edge.

The Executioner would have to watch his ass, and no mistake.

He marked the spot and went to find the fence, three strands of razor wire that would do more to stop a deer than a determined infiltrator. He hadn't been told which section of his beat to cover first, and so he chose the left at random, moving slowly, silently to westward, following the wire. With starlight to assist him, walking unfamiliar woodland, Bolan estimated that five hundred yards should take him anywhere from twenty minutes to a half an hour, one-way, if he met no obstacles. Call it three round-trips on his beat, before his shift was over for the night.

He was concerned about the possibility of ambush, but concern and fear were very different things. This time around he had a rifle and 120 rounds of 5.56 mm ammunition going for him, and the faceless enemy had to know that he was armed. Would that prevent a new attack this night, or was the would-be killer so determined that he couldn't wait? Whoever was behind the shooting incident, Lou Doyle or someone else, had to know that Pike and Stone were on the warpath, aching for a chance to chew somebody out. Before he ran the risk of death at Bolan's hand or discipline by the militia, the elusive enemy would need sufficient motivation to proceed.

And Bolan wondered if a broken nose would be enough to do the trick.

An hour's cautious walking put him back where he had started, moving toward the east wing of his beat. He had seen nothing of the other sentries on his first round, and there was no reason why he should. A thousand yards of darkened woodland was a lot for any single man to cover adequately, but the lookouts were assisted by the fact that they had no fixed schedule. An intruder couldn't plan his penetration based on sentry movements, if a guard might turn up here, there, anywhere, at any given time.

Bolan had no idea what kind of problems Pike and company had had with prowlers in the past, nor did he care. Admittedly he spent more time watching his back more than checking out the wire. His two priorities were the completion of his mission and survival, in that order. At the moment his devotion to the turn at guard duty was limited to making sure his cover held.

If anyone came looking for him in the darkness, they would have to take their chances with the Executioner.

He had covered twenty yards or so on round two of his beat before he heard the noise, no more than fifty feet in front of him. It could have been a deer, but Bolan didn't think so.

It was a myth that forest dwellers always moved in perfect silence. Any woodsman who has heard a deer or squirrel in flight could readily attest to that. If sight, sound and smell revealed no predators or prey in the vicinity, most animals were just as prone to sneezing, farting, scratching, yawning, crunching leaves or twigs as any human being.

This sound was different, though. It was the kind of noise a furtive individual would make by accident, immediately followed by dead silence. Bolan's mind produced a snap-shot of the prowler, hunched in shadow, straining eyes and ears against the night and praying there was no one close enough to hear.

A stalker from outside? he wondered. Or somebody from the compound, creeping out to find him? If the latter, was the person friend or foe? Some field commanders made a point of trying to surprise their sentries, catch them with their guard down, maybe even sleeping on the job. He didn't know Pike well enough to say if that would be his style, but anything was possible. Conversely, if the shooter from the recent war games was about to make his second try, a lackadaisical response on Bolan's part could be his last.

It was impossible to fix with any certainty upon a single sound, but if the prowler slipped again—

Like that!

Bolan started forward, taking care to make no sounds himself. Whoever had made the noise had to be close now. Bolan kept a tight rein on his own imagination, knowing how the darkness and a case of nerves could make the rustle of a windblown leaf sound like a marching rifle company, the night call of a cricket sound like weapons being cocked. He took his time, not dawdling but not rushing, either, making up his mind to get it right the first time.

A muted scuffling sound from Bolan's right took him in that direction, moving farther from the fence. He crouched beside a looming oak and waited for the night to show him something out of place: a glint of metal in the starlight, perspiration on the prowler's face.

There!

A gentle breeze was blowing from the north, but now he saw a shadow moving stealthily against the wind. Another moment, and it took on human shape. The size was difficult to judge, stooped over as the prowler was, all dressed in black, but Bolan pegged his weight somewhere around 150 pounds. If he was armed, the weapon wasn't showing. Still, the Executioner would take no chances. It would make no sense at all for unarmed, black-clad strangers to be creeping through the woods out here, on private property, inside a barbed-wire fence.

But if the night crawler had come for Bolan, if he knew where Bolan was supposed to be on watch, why was he headed back in the direction of the camp?

A long stride brought him up behind the prowler, close enough to touch. He could have killed the stranger with a minimum of effort—clubbed him with the rifle, shot him, snapped his neck or cut his throat—but Bolan hesitated, just in case it *was* a test of Pike's or Stone's, in case a death wasn't required.

Instead, he kicked the prowler squarely in the backside, heard a startled *woof!* as the dark figure staggered forward, flattening against the rough bark of a pine. Bolan was on him in a flash, twisting one arm behind the prowler's back with force enough to bring a grunt of pain, his free hand searching for a weapon. A pistol holstered on a leather belt was removed and tucked in Bolan's waistband while the stranger—smaller than he had originally estimated—struggled helplessly against the arm lock. Bolan reached around to check for other weapons and was startled as his fingers cupped a round, firm breast.

"God*damn* you!"

Kicking backward, his assailant missed her target, barely grazing Bolan's outer thigh. He took advantage of the moment, hooked a heel inside the leg that bore her weight and brought the woman to her knees. A brisk shove jammed her face against the tree as Bolan whipped her other arm around behind her back.

"You bastard!"

"Flattery will get you nowhere," Bolan said.

"You're in a lot of trouble, mister."

"I'd say it's the other way around."

With one hand pinning both slim wrists, he held her fast and drew the pistol from his belt, applied its muzzle to the soft skin of her neck, below the rolled edge of a black watch cap.

"Who sent you?" Bolan asked.

"As if you didn't know."

He thumbed back the pistol's hammer. "Is this the way you want to play it?"

"I'd think twice if I were you." The woman's voice was shaky, she was breathing hard, but she had guts to spare. "One federal agent, you might pull it off. But two..."

A Fed?

"I'll need ID," he said.

"That's my line."

"And a warrant," Bolan added. "You're trespassing on private property."

"So sue me."

"You don't need a lawyer. You need a miracle."

He let her go, stepped back and put the gun away. The lady turned to face him, one hand rising to her forehead, where a dark smudge could have passed for dirt or blood.

"Go on, then," she defied him. "Do it!"

"What's the magic word?"

"Fuck you!" she said. "How's that? You bastards killed my partner, so don't expect me to come begging. If you plan to shoot me, get it over with."

"I haven't made my mind up yet," he said.

"Hey, take your time. It gives my backup time to get here."

"Call them," Bolan told her.

She hesitated, thinking. "What?"

"You heard me. Give a yell. The more the merrier."

She glared at Bolan, making no reply. He watched her for another moment, making up his mind.

"I think we'd better have a talk," he said at last.

7

"Say what?"

The federal agent's expression told him that she would have burst out laughing under different circumstances—if they had been talking, for example, in a place where she wasn't so likely to be killed. The present atmosphere ruled out frivolity, however, and inhibited the lady from raising her voice.

"You heard me right."

"Ah. So *you're* a federal officer? Just by coincidence?"

"This meeting's a coincidence," he replied, "but you created it. You're not supposed to be here."

"And you are." The skepticism fairly dripped from every word she spoke.

"That's right."

"Uh-huh." She crossed her arms and stared at Bolan, her expression almost sullen. "Fine," she said at last. "What agency?"

"You're not familiar with it," Bolan told her.

"Really. I suppose it's need-to-know?"

"Something like that," he said.

"Wow, I'm impressed." She made a sour face. "So tell me, does this bullshit work where you come from? Do women eat it up, regardless of the situation? Are you living in the Twilight Zone, or what?"

"You'd better take this," Bolan said, handing back the

pistol he had lifted from her holster. "You'll be needing it if you don't learn to keep your voice down."

He was gambling big time, and he knew it. There was nothing to prevent the lady from shooting him and taking off, nothing except the innate curiosity that he had tweaked with his remarks before he handed back the gun.

She swiftly checked the weapon's magazine and chamber, making sure he hadn't secretly unloaded it or something when her back was turned. That done, she thumbed the hammer back, but didn't point the gun at Bolan, holding it against her thigh, its muzzle pointed toward the ground.

"Don't shoot yourself," he cautioned.

"Don't concern yourself!" she snapped.

"That's right," he said, "I guess they train you pretty well at ATF."

She blinked three times at that before she caught herself and simply glared. Suspiciously she said, "I never told you who I work for."

Bolan shrugged. "I took a shot."

In fact he had dipped into Hal Brognola's file for something he could use, remembering the two Feds who had disappeared while working the militia case. From this one's visible reaction, Bolan guessed it wasn't such a long shot, after all.

"So, now you're psychic, too?"

"Laugh all you want," he said. "Smart money says you're Ginger Ross, eight years with ATF, two commendations on the job, officially AWOL for ten days now. Your partner, Jeffrey Donald Frasier—"

"Jeff," she interrupted him in a little-girl voice, wounded to the heart. "I call him Jeff."

"Jeff Frasier disappeared while working undercover on the Paul Revere Militia. Four days after he lost contact, you dropped off the screen. About this time the brass is wondering if they should have a double funeral or give your partner a memorial and can your ass for playing out of bounds.''

"You couldn't know all that," Ross said. "Not even if you tortured Jeff. You couldn't know the rest of it. My name, okay, but not... Who are you, anyway?"

"Belasko," Bolan told her. "Mike Belasko. And I never saw your partner. Truth is, I just got here yesterday myself."

"That doesn't tell me who you work for."

"No," he said, "it doesn't."

"Great. Some kind of cloak-and-dagger crap, is that the game? You know chapter and verse about me, but you're the great enigma? Sorry, I don't play that way."

"You weren't invited," Bolan told her.

"What's that supposed to mean?"

"You're out of line, with people looking for you. At the very least, you owe them a report. I understand your motivation—"

"Do you really?"

"But there's nothing you can do alone, unless you want to raise the body count by turning into a statistic."

"So, they sent you out to bring me back."

"Not me," he replied. "You don't figure in my plans at all."

"I'm sure."

"The ATF cleans up its own mess," Bolan said, resisting the temptation to remark that they had had a lot of practice in the past few years. "My only interest in your game is that it interferes with *my* assignment."

"Ah. Which is?"

"As you expected—need-to-know. Back off."

"Like hell!" she said. "These bastards killed my partner. How am I supposed to let that go?"

He wondered briefly if there had been something personal between the lady and Frasier, something more than the near-blood connection longtime partners often formed in law-enforcement work. It was a possibility, of course, but Bolan didn't have the time to speculate.

"It's being taken care of," he advised her.

"Oh? How's that? You're taking care of it? Is that what I'm supposed to think."

"I frankly don't care what you think."

"So, chivalry *is* dead."

"If you want knights in shining armor," Bolan told her, "check out a Renaissance festival. This is the real world, as down and dirty as it gets."

"I guess I'm supposed to thank you, right? Is this the part where I get misty-eyed with gratitude?"

"This is the part where you get moving," Bolan said. "While you still can."

"Threats, now?"

"Not even close," he said. "You came in here to find the men who took your partner out, correct?"

"Damn right."

"Okay. Assume you found them. Forty-odd commandos armed with automatic weapons, ammo up the ass. What did you plan to do with *that?*" As Bolan spoke, he nodded toward the semiauto pistol in her hand.

"I'm not a vigilante," she replied defensively. "I was looking for evidence, dammit!"

"Uh-huh." He didn't even try to hide his skepticism. "I imagine there's a ton of it lying around the compound. And your warrant's up-to-date, of course."

"If I go back and play it by the book, they'll put me on a desk."

"As well they should," he said. "You're too damn close."

"Somebody had to pay for what they did to Jeff!"

"Somebody will," he promised her.

"Oh, right. So, what's the plan? A RICO violation? Maybe take another shot at the sedition angle? Hell, why not? It worked so well the last time."

"Listen, neither one of us has time to stand around debating how some prosecutor blew a game ten years ago. I had no part in that, and you weren't even on the job. The smart thing, if you want to keep that job, would be for you to call your boss and think of some good explanation for the past ten days."

"No, thanks."

"Your call," he said, "but you're not coming into camp tonight."

"Says who?"

He shifted slightly to remind her of the automatic rifle in his hands. "Says me."

"Oh, yeah?"

"I've got a cover to protect," he said. "If push comes to shove, you'd give me up. The other way, who knows? I might get a promotion."

He was bluffing, but the lady had no way of knowing that. "Did anybody ever tell you you're a bastard?" she inquired.

"It rings a bell."

"You spin this bullshit line, and I'm supposed to walk away, pretend that nothing's happened."

He could see her knuckles blanching as she clutched the gun more tightly. If he couldn't give her something, there was still a chance that she might try to drop him where he stood, before she made her break in one direction or the other.

"How's your memory?" he asked.

"Excuse me?"

"There's a number you can call in Washington. Explain your situation. Give my name. They'll verify my story."

"And report me to the ATF," she said. "You think I'm stupid?"

"Use a pay phone," Bolan said. "Hell, grab a transient off the street and have him make the call. Use some initiative."

"That's what I'm doing here tonight," she said.

"Wrong time, wrong place."

She glared at Bolan for another moment, then eased down the hammer on her pistol and returned it to the holster on her hip.

"So, what's the number."

Bolan gave her the ten digits, nodding to himself as she repeated them. It was a cutout number that would patch her through to Stony Man Farm, with a potential link to Hal Brognola's office, if required. The combination of his cover name and certain private data to confirm her own ID would free up enough sanitized information to convince her that another agency was on the Paul Revere Militia's case. As to the point of whether she would be appeased, well, Bolan wouldn't be inclined to bet the farm on that.

The lady had determination, undercover work had taught her how to break the rules and she was righteously pissed off. If there was—had been—a romantic interest in her partner, that introduced a whole new range of volatile and unpredictable emotions. Bolan was hoping that didn't turn out to be the case, then caught himself and wondered why he even cared.

The job.

Of course, that had to be the answer. Getting even for a murdered partner was one thing, a motive he could work with, something the professionals at Justice could defuse with any luck. But getting even for a lover's death could elevate the lady's actions to the status of an all-out holy war.

"I'll make the call," she told him grudgingly. "No promises, you understand?"

"I hear you," Bolan said.

"If I find out you're jerking me around on this, some kind of bullshit story, I'll be coming back for you."

"Fair's fair."

"Meantime, if you find out what happened to my partner—"

"I'll relay the word through channels," Bolan told her.

"Great. Did anybody ever tell you you're all heart?"

"Not recently," he said.

"There's a surprise."

He trailed her to the fence and watched her stoop, slip through the strands of razor wire with practiced ease, as agile as an acrobat. A moment later she was gone without a backward glance.

This was all he needed to compound the difficulty of his mission. Bolan stood and listened to the night, sounds of Ross retreating in the darkness, fading out entirely after several moments. There was still a chance that she would circle back and try some other point on the perimeter, but Bolan didn't think so.

Not tonight.

As for tomorrow...

Bolan sympathized with her. Most of his own life had been spent outside "the System," more or less, pursuing private justice against ruthless predators in human form. He couldn't fault the lady there, but she had picked the worst time possible to make her move from Bolan's point of view. There were enough wild cards already in the game, with Pike and Stone, Lou Doyle, an unknown shooter skulking in the forest. On top of everything, he would be wanted by a certain sheriff in Montana now, for roughing up the deputies in Laurin. If the lady Fed began to put her two cents in, the whole damn set could fall apart.

He didn't want to see her harmed—far from it. Bolan could admire her courage and determination, praise her sense of duty to a fallen partner, but he also recognized that Ginger Ross lacked preparation for the game she had in mind. There was a world of difference between investigating suspects, even infiltrating outlaw groups, and waging a guerrilla war outside the law. The lady Fed was trained to gather evidence, observe, report and prosecute. Her education in the art of dealing death was limited to self-defense, the kind of situations where an inch-thick book of laws and bureaucratic guidelines authorized the use of deadly force.

The Executioner had come to his profession by a different route, with different rules. Unleashed against an enemy in wartime, he was trained to raise as much hell as he could, by any means at his disposal, sometimes spotting isolated targets, other times annihilating anything that moved. He understood the legal rules of evidence, the way a surgeon may be technically conversant with diesel mechanics, knowing that the details have no relevance, no impact on his stock-in-trade. The White House didn't call Brognola, and Brognola didn't summon Bolan, if the plan involved a bad guy being sent to jail.

He was the court of last resort, a specialist in surgical removal of the enemy when all else failed. The targets Bolan drew were too much for the law to handle; they were legally or diplomatically untouchable, immune to prosecution with their fortunes, batteries of lawyers or the sixth sense that permitted them to stay one step ahead of federal manhunters. When greed or madness elevated them above the level of danger posed by thugs and terrorists, a more aggressive treatment program was devised. Its emphasis was on eradication of malignancy. The patients weren't expected to survive.

He took a deep breath, held it for a moment, willing himself to relax. There was nothing more that he could do about Ginger Ross at the moment, no way to warn Brognola or protect himself beyond the steps he had already taken. If she called the cutout number, Stony Man and Brognola would run with it the best they could. If she decided not to play...

His mind ran down the possibilities as he continued on his way, still going through the motions on his post. In one scenario—the best, from Bolan's point of view—a trace enabled Stony Man or someone from the ATF to drop a net on Ross for her own protection, hold her in debriefing for a week or so, until he saw his mission wrapped up, one way or another. That would be ideal, and since it was ideal, Bolan was wise enough to know it likely wouldn't happen.

In another version, equally at odds with logic, Ross skipped the call but finally decided on her own to come in from the cold, let someone else pursue her partner's murderers. She could beg forgiveness, maybe take a short suspension, and get on with her career while Bolan did his job.

Fat chance.

The lady had impressed him with her zeal, which meant that she wouldn't give up because of one brief conversation with a total stranger. Quite the opposite, in fact—if she imagined she was being stonewalled, she would be more likely to proceed without official sanction, bent on seeing justice done at any cost.

The trouble, Bolan told himself, was that she didn't understand what that could mean. Even if Ross was resolved to using force, a part of her would still expect to find the smoking gun and drag her adversaries into court. She had been on the job quite long enough to recognize the difference between life and art. She wasn't Lady Rambo, and her outrage at the murder of her partner didn't qualify her as a one-woman guerrilla force.

If he pursued the matter, though, she would inevitably reach a point where rules went out the window and she had to play for keeps. She had already risked her life by coming to the compound on her own without a warrant after dark. It was dumb luck that she had stumbled into Bolan rather than some other sentry who would probably have killed her on the spot.

He hoped that scare would slow her down, but Bolan knew he couldn't count on it. The lucky break might even drive her to another, even more reckless attempt, believing that she had a friend inside the camp who would protect her when the chips were down.

If she came back, he knew, the odds were fifty-fifty that she would be killed or captured. As a prisoner, she could betray him now, blow Bolan's cover with a few words to her captors. Not that she would mean to, but federal agents weren't instructed in the fine art of resisting torture or chemical interrogation. In their world *they* asked all the questions, while the suspects either spilled their guts or lawyered up and bit their tongues.

It was a whole new ball game on the dark side of the moon.

Instead of dwelling on a problem that defied solution, Bolan made a conscious shift to reassess his first day with the Paul Reveres. He was inside, with several friends, at least one enemy and nothing solid on the terrorist connection. It was asking too much to expect that anyone would spill his guts to him this soon, but he was hopeful. If his cover held, if he was able to promote himself with Pike and Stone, if he could keep himself from getting killed by Doyle or whoever was stalking him, he might just have a shot.

At what?

He started from the premise that Brognola was correct, and that the Paul Reveres were practicing domestic terrorism. Pike and Stone were at the root of it, but he wasn't prepared to drop them yet, until he understood exactly how the network functioned. It would do no good if he removed the serpent's head, only to watch the body disintegrate, each piece wriggling off in a separate direction to carry on as before.

He had to get it right the first time, since he might not have a second chance.

The time passed slowly on his beat, but Bolan settled into it, remembering the more immediate risk from persons unknown in the compound, watching his back as he had before Ginger Ross appeared to distract him. There were different ways to die in Bolan's world, but the result would be identical, regardless of the means.

Come midnight, he was waiting for the duty sergeant at the point where they had parted company six hours earlier. The jeep had three more sleepy-looking soldiers in it, one of them unloading to take Bolan's place.

"No problems?" the sergeant asked, as they pulled away.

"A couple of raccoons," Bolan replied. "Nothing that I couldn't handle."

"Nobody tried to shoot you?" someone asked behind him.

Bolan swiveled in his seat to face the speaker—Cartwright, from the mess hall. From the woods, that afternoon.

"Not this time," Bolan said with a smile. "Maybe the shooter got his nose out of joint."

8

Winnemucca was a wide spot in the road, a one-time trading post along Nevada's Humboldt River, now a town of sorts on U.S. Highway 80. As the seat of Humboldt County, it laid claim to some four thousand full-time residents, but that was fudging it, including some who lived outside the city limits, in the desert thereabouts. The town was a dusty wide spot in the road, but not without attractions, all the same.

If you'd been driving through Nevada's northern wasteland for a few hot, grueling hours—headed north from Sparks and Reno, say, or west from Elko—Winnemucca looked like paradise, or possibly the next best thing. It offered filling stations, restaurants, a theater, motels, some gambling if you hadn't had your fill or been cleaned out before you got that far. A mile or so due north, on Highway 95, you'd even find a whorehouse—trailers, really, drawn up in a circle like a wagon train awaiting hostile Indians—which was entirely legal under the Nevada county-option rule.

And Winnemucca had a bank.

You might expect Stockman's Commerce Bank of Winnemucca to be small potatoes, and it surely looked that way from the outside. Constructed in the Great Depression and essentially unmodified since then, the bank was a two-story structure, brick and concrete, with a vault on the ground floor. Decorators had been in a time or two since 1935 to spruce up the interior, but it still had a homey feel about it.

Appearances could be deceiving, though, and Winnemucca's bank, while modest in its physical dimensions, did a booming business with the local entertainment industry—casinos and saloons—as well as Humboldt County ranchers who were big in sheep and cotton. Published assets hovered in the neighborhood of twenty-five or thirty million dollars, with some ten or twelve percent of that available in cash on any given day.

Thursday was best for what he had in mind, Chris Stone decided, since the stores would probably be paying off their staff on Friday, and the fleshpots would be stocking up on cash to get them through the weekend. Thursday also meant that the bank had been collecting its deposits since the Open sign went up on Monday morning and the regulars began unloading money they had made since the previous Friday afternoon.

His team drove south on Highway 96 from Oregon: three cars, eight men. They didn't run in tandem, like a military caravan, but spaced it out, fifteen or twenty minutes in between. The cars were stolen, and the license plates had come from other cars, collected over six or seven months in several states. Stone's Nissan Pathfinder had California plates; the Dodge Intrepid seemed to come from Washington; the Chevy Lumina had Arizona tags. Each driver watched the speed limit, did nothing to excite highway patrolmen or invite a traffic stop. If anything came down along the way, the guns were out of sight but readily available.

The plan was no extravaganza, since he liked to keep things simple when he could, but Stone had worked it out in detail. On a weekday afternoon there should be something like a dozen cops on duty, counting constables, the sheriff's men and one or two highway patrolmen operating from the county seat. In any kind of stand-up fight, Stone had a feeling his eight men could handle it, but he was looking for an edge, not for a massacre. Distraction was the key, and on his first dry run through Winnemucca three weeks earlier, he had devised the perfect scheme.

They needed something that would draw the uniforms away from Stockman's Commerce Bank while Stone and company were making their withdrawal, something to keep the piglets hopping while a team of crack professionals went in, scooped up the cash and split.

Something like an explosion, for example. Maybe more than one.

And so, three cars. The Dodge would be proceeding west, through town, when they arrived, and it would make two stops before it doubled back on Highway 80, rolling eastward, 125 miles to Elko, where it would pick up Highway 225 north to Idaho and home. Along the way it would be ditched somewhere, new wheels acquired, clean plates applied for the return trip to the compound.

Stone and three companions in the Pathfinder, meanwhile, would wait until the fireworks started, then complete their business at Stockman's Commerce Bank while local officers were otherwise engaged. The Chevy was their crash car, just in case. Its occupants had drawn straws for the honor, and the losers had been righteously angry when they were left behind.

Good men, for what he had in mind. But they still weren't soldiers.

Never mind.

This was payday for the Paul Revere Militia, and it wouldn't hurt Stone, either. If the job went smoothly, certain people would be very pleased.

"I OUGHT TO BE with Stone and them inside the bank," Lou Doyle repeated for the sixth or seventh time since they had left Burns Junction, Oregon, around the crack of dawn. "I don't deserve this shit."

"It's an important job," Jack Cartwright told him, riding in the Dodge's shotgun seat and staring out at the Joshua trees and cactus sprouting up like headstones in the middle of the desert.

"Grunt work," Doyle informed him sourly. "Somebody else could do it. You could do it."

"I am doing it." You'd think Doyle was an idiot, sometimes, the way he couldn't see the obvious.

"Alone, I mean," Doyle snapped at him. "Or with somebody else."

"Could be they didn't want to strain you," Cartwright answered, "with your injury and all."

"Is that supposed to be a joke, asshole?" Behind the wide strip of adhesive tape, Doyle's face had turned a darker shade of red. "You think it's funny?"

Cartwright slipped a hand inside his windbreaker to touch the .45 with the extended magazine. Doyle had a temper on him, sure enough, but he was flesh and blood like anybody else.

"You see me laughing?" he replied.

"I'd better not."

"You need to concentrate on business," Cartwright reminded him. "You can take care of what's-his-name when we get back."

"Belasko. Smart bastard figures he can make me take his shit and like it, he's in for a big surprise."

"Whatever. Let's just handle first things first, okay?"

"You don't think I can handle this?"

"I'm saying we should concentrate, that's all."

"Smart bastard."

Cartwright didn't know if Doyle meant him or Belasko, and didn't care. Doyle's mission was to drive the car, watch out for uniforms and keep a cool head on his shoulders in the process. That would be the hard part, Cartwright realized. Doyle was always getting pissed off about one thing or another, living in a constant state of agitation over some imagined insult.

Not that much imagination was required this time. The new kid on the block had kicked Doyle's ass in front of twenty-five or thirty witnesses, and the men could never let that rest. His first attempt at payback had gone sour, landing Rick Guarini on his back in the infirmary, but Doyle was hanging tough. When Stone and Colonel Pike had questioned him about the shooting, Doyle had played it cool for once and shined them on, as if he were trying out for an Academy Award. The other members of his team, all friends, had backed him up and sworn that they were nowhere near the spot where Guarini was hit.

Strike one.

That night, when they were changing shifts on watch, Cartwright couldn't resist goading Belasko just a little, but the way the new guy came right back at him, that line about the shooter's nose, told Cartwright that he knew what was going on. Things had been quiet for the next two days, until they took off on the present job, and he was wishing Doyle could let it go.

Which was about as likely as a dinosaur appearing in the middle of the highway, wearing a bikini while it played a saxophone.

Approaching Winnemucca, Cartwright brought his mind back to the job at hand. A metal lunch pail sat under the driver's seat, gray and unremarkable. Another, this one stainless steel, was on the floor behind the driver's seat. From all appearances, they were a pair of average wage slaves on their way to work. A cop would have to look inside the lunch pails to discover otherwise, and he would never live that long.

Each lunch box held three pounds of C-4 plastique, with a battery secured inside the lid where you would normally expect to find a thermos bottle. A simple kitchen timer was rigged up to the detonator. Neither bomb was armed, right now, but that would only take a moment once they reached their destination and were ready to begin.

Cartwright checked his watch and saw that they were right on time. Of course. One thing about Lou Doyle, when he had orders to perform a certain job, he followed those instructions to the letter. He might bitch about it going in or afterward, but he would always be on time, connect the dots, go through the necessary motions. You could call him seven kinds of asshole and be right on every count, but no one ever called him lazy or suggested he was letting down the side.

"That's it," Cartwright said, pointing to the smallish Saddle West Casino. "Over there."

"I see it."

Cartwright had never been to Winnemucca in his life, but he had studied all the maps until he reckoned he could find his way around the county like a native. All things considered, it should be a piece of cake.

Doyle parked around one side of the casino and left the engine running, with the shift in neutral. Cartwright took the lunch pail from behind Doyle's seat and opened it, reaching in to set the timer for eleven minutes. At their next stop he would make it eight or nine, depending on how long it took for them to get there.

"See you in a minute," he told his companion, expecting no reply and getting none.

The Saddle West was cool and dark inside, like every other gambling house Cartwright had ever seen. They wanted the players nice and comfy, no distractions to remind them whether it was day or night outside, no clocks in evidence. The place was sparsely populated at that hour, getting on toward noon, and no one gave a second glance to Cartwright as he turned left past the bar and proceeded toward the men's room. Once inside, he checked out the stalls, confirmed that he was all alone and set the loaded lunch box on the middle toilet out of three. He locked the stall from the inside, to keep it more or less secure, and scrambled over the partition in a flash, making his exit through the stall next door.

No sweat.

The barkeep had his back turned, rinsing glasses, as Cartwright made his second pass. Somebody might have seen him, granted. There was no way to avoid that if he didn't wear a mask, which would have made him pretty damn conspicuous. He knew from television and the movies that eyewitness testimony was the least reliable of any evidence, no matter what the average man or woman on the street might think. In the confusion of the blast, if people remembered him at all, they were as likely to produce irrelevant descriptions as to make his face. Besides, he'd never been arrested, and the cops would have a hard time tracking down a recent photograph.

Outside, the sun was waiting for him, bright and hot. Doyle watched him through windshield glare as he approached the Dodge, a sour expression on his face.

"One down," Cartwright said as he slid into the shotgun seat, "and one to go."

THE CALL CAUGHT Sheriff Arnold Dunstan by surprise. That was uncommon, after everything that he had seen in thirty-seven years of law enforcement, but it still could happen now and then. The first report of an explosion at the Saddle West Casino had been vague, one of the barmaids sounding half-hysterical, but Dunstan got the gist of it and had his dispatcher beam an all-cars-out for every man on duty, plus a call to the fire department and the paramedics.

Smoke was everywhere when he arrived, lights winking from the rack atop his cruiser as he bailed out and moved through the haze toward the casino. It was nothing to compare with any of the carpet joints in Reno, much less Vegas, but the owner made a decent living, fleecing tourists when he could and letting locals win enough that they kept coming back for more. As far as Dunstan knew—and he knew most of what went on in Winnemucca, one way or another—the proprietor, if not beloved in the community, at least had no one on his shit list who would want to bomb him off the map.

It didn't have to be a bomb, of course. It could have been a gas line going off, maybe a leaking propane tank. But this was different. Dunstan could see that something had exploded through the south wall of the building, scattering debris across the parking lot and smashing windows out of half a dozen cars. It didn't seem to Dunstan that the place was burning, more like smoke was drifting outward from the source of the explosion.

What the hell had happened here?

A group of people stood outside the main casino entrance: Tim the bartender, with blood smeared on his face, two cocktail waitresses in skimpy Pocahontas costumes, the Mexican cook and half a dozen locals who were either in the club or passing by when it blew up. Dunstan would have to question each of them in turn, or let his men help. Approaching sirens told him help was on the way. A few more minutes, and—

The new blast wasn't close, like right around the corner, but it wasn't all that far away. In Winnemucca no two points were all that widely separated, when you really thought about it. Turning toward the sound of the explosion, somewhere to the west, Dunstan could see another smoke cloud rising, dark against the washed-out desert sky.

A second blast meant that it couldn't be an accident. No way at all. But what, then?

Dunstan heard the two-way radio in his cruiser squawking, the dispatcher wanting him to pick up in a hurry. Cursing underneath his breath at forces he couldn't begin to understand right now, the sheriff turned and ran back toward his car.

"MAKE SURE YOU KEEP the engine running."

"Right."

Another wheelman might have been insulted by the terse reminder, but it didn't seem to phase young Eddie Cole. Stone liked that quality in his subordinates, submissiveness without the full-scale leap into servility that made them seem like lapdogs waiting for a treat. Good soldiers, even amateurs, accepted orders without question, and they didn't flare up over nothing in the crunch.

Stone crossed the sunbaked asphalt with determined strides. He didn't have to check to know the others were behind him, Hicks and Schaefer, bringing up the rear and sticking close. Before he reached the front doors of Stockman's Commerce Bank, Stone had on his ski mask, knew Hicks and Schaefer would be similarly masked.

They all wore Kevlar bulletproof vests under nylon windbreakers and carried MGP-84 submachine guns, the Minis, 11.2 inches long with the stocks folded, 6.4 pounds with 32-round magazines in place. The Peruvian-made SMGs were compact and efficient, chambered in 9 mm, with a cyclic rate of fire approaching 700 rounds per minute in full-auto mode. They could accommodate suppressors if the muzzle caps were first removed, but Stone cared nothing about noise this day. If anything went wrong inside the bank, he was prepared to rock and roll.

On Stone's first trip to Winnemucca, he had checked the bank and found out that it closed for lunch from noon to one o'clock each day. With that in mind, he had arranged to cross the threshold at 11:55 a.m., when there would be less risk of meeting any customers. Stone didn't care if someone wound up getting hurt or wasted in the raid, but every individual they had to deal with added risk to the equation. Fewer hostages meant fewer possibilities that something would go wrong.

A fifty-something guard was walking toward the front doors as they entered, blinking at the men with guns and reaching for the pistol on his hip. Stone rushed the rent-a-cop and swung his Mini in a vicious arc, connecting with his adversary's cheek. Blood spurted from a jagged gash that showed bone white beneath the open flesh, then the rent-a-cop was down. Stone snatched his pistol from its holster, slipped the piece into his belt and kept on moving toward the tellers' cages, knowing Hicks and Schaefer had his back.

"Heads up!" he shouted to the startled bank employees, three young women and a chunky, balding man who had to be the manager. "There's two ways we can do this. If you follow orders, nobody gets hurt. You wanna be heroic, they can put it on your tombstone, but if one goes, everybody goes. What'll it be?"

The bald man had his hands raised overhead. "Take anything you want," he said, "but please don't shoot."

"That's what I like to hear," Stone said. "Everybody down, now. Kiss the floor!"

When they were lined up at his feet, Stone turned to Hicks and Schaefer, saw that one of them had turned the sign on the front door around to indicate the bank was closed.

"Let's get it done," he said. "I've got the lobby. Skip the drawers and clear the vault."

Even a hick-town bank would have security devices standing by in the event of robbery. The ceiling-mounted cameras couldn't pierce their masks, but many cash drawers came equipped with pressure plates or other sensors that would sound alarms if certain bills were moved, explosive dye packs—it could be anything. He could afford to pass the several hundred dollars sitting in the drawers in favor of the real loot waiting for him in the vault.

Stone watched the clock while Hicks and Schaefer disappeared into the strong room, hauling folded duffel bags from underneath their windbreakers. When they emerged two minutes later on the dot, both bags were full and dragging down their shoulders with the weight of bundled cash inside.

Payday.

"We're out of here," he told the four employees stretched out on the floor. "I've got a man across the street to watch our backs. If any uniforms show up in the next ten minutes, he's got orders to start bagging blue-suits on the spot. Stay cool, and you'll be all right."

It was a load of bullshit, but it just might work. Assuming someone called the cops before his deadline, though, they would be stalled while uniforms were beckoned from the bombing scenes. And if worse came to worst, he had two men in the crash car, standing by to cover his retreat.

Outside he stripped off his mask as he jogged toward the Pathfinder. Another moment, and the vehicle was rolling east through downtown Winnemucca toward the city limits and the great wasteland beyond.

"How about some air-conditioning?" Schaefer asked from the back.

"Sure thing," Eddie Cole said, already stretching out a hand to the controls.

Stone felt the cold air blowing on his sweaty face and smiled. It felt like he did.

Nice and cool.

"THEY SHOULD BE DONE by now," Cartwright said.

Doyle glanced at the Intrepid's dashboard clock and nodded to himself. If everything went smoothly, Chris Stone and the others should be on the road.

And if it fell apart, well, there was nothing Doyle could do about it, was there? He had done his part, right by the numbers. It was all that anyone could logically expect.

The Dodge was ten miles east of town, on U.S. 80, rolling at a steady sixty-five. No violation there, since they had raised the speed limits. With so much nothing all around him, Doyle could probably have driven ninety miles per hour without drawing any notice, but he didn't want to take the chance. If anything went wrong on this job, it wasn't about to be his fault.

He still had business to take care of at the compound, and the thought of Mike Belasko waiting for him, still alive and well, made Doyle more anxious to get back. His palms itched with the need to wrap both hands around Belasko's neck and squeeze until his face turned black, his eyes bugged out and there was no life left in him at all.

It wouldn't be that easy, though. The bastard had already proved that much, not once, but twice. He had quick hands, and it was difficult to take him by surprise.

Okay. So be it.

Difficult wasn't *impossible*. They were two different things entirely, as Lou Doyle had good and ample cause to understand. If he could only keep his wits about him, take it nice and slow, he would be able to devise a foolproof plan and put the new boy in his place.

Hell, put him in his grave.

It couldn't be like last time, though. It had been close, that one, Stone and Pike all over him with questions. Any member of his red team could have blown it for him—one word out of place, and he could only guess at what the colonel might have done in terms of discipline.

No, that was too damn risky. Next time out he had to set the stage just right, make sure Belasko walked into a trap that could be blamed on someone else, outside the compound. That would mean Doyle had to wait and bide his time, but he could handle it. Before he was a fighting patriot, he'd been a hunter, stalking deer and anything else that crossed his rifle sights in the woods of his native Michigan. Hunting took patience if you did it properly.

He knew the game, and he could wait.

Belasko wasn't going anywhere. Not yet. And when he went, he would be going all the way.

Doyle switched on the radio, fiddling with it until he

found a country-western station, old Merle Haggard, telling some woman that she didn't have to call him "Darling" if she didn't want to.

Good enough.

He had a long drive back to camp in which to plan his next move in a very private war.

And next time, Doyle determined, he would get it right.

9

The phone call settled nothing, as far as Ginger Ross was concerned. She actually had to try the number twice before she found out anything—if you could call it that. The first time she had barely gotten started, barely gave them Mike Belasko's name—assuming that it was his name—when the young woman on the other end had asked if she could hold.

Hell, no.

Ross had been around the business long enough to know about phone traces. Everything was faster these days, with computers and the other tricks technicians used. The Caller ID system printed out a number when you dialed; they didn't even have to answer at the other end to know where you were calling from. Even a mobile telephone could get you busted if the opposition had triangulation gear.

The number he had given her was in Connecticut—Norwich, according to the area code—but what did that really mean these days? With cutouts, they could bounce the call back and forth across the country through relays in nothing flat. She might be talking to an operator in D.C. or California, and she wouldn't know the difference. The odds were in her favor, though, that they weren't in Idaho, which gave her time.

Not much, but some.

Instead of hanging on the line, Ross had told her nameless contact that she would be calling back inside the hour, and expected certain answers to be waiting for her when she did. The second time around she used a different public telephone—drove twenty miles, in fact, to make the damn call from a different town—and she hadn't been disappointed.

Just confused.

A man had picked up when she called the second time, but he knew all about her first call, and he did his best to back up Mike Belasko's story. Most of it was covert operations, need-to-know, and blah-blah-blah, but by the time she cradled the receiver, Ross had begun to wonder what in hell was going on.

It wasn't ATF; she knew that much, though Treasury might be involved somehow, around the fringes. FBI? She doubted it. The Bureau liked its secrets too much to be giving anything away by telephone. They wouldn't talk to Ross's supervisors half the time, much less to some rogue agent who was AWOL in the field and calling up to grill them on the mission of an undercover agent.

Who, then?

Ross didn't flatter herself into thinking that she was important enough to rate that kind of operation. If she had been, if Belasko was looking for her in the Paul Revere compound, then he would have bagged her when he had the chance. Still, he had known about her partner, knew his middle name, for Christ's sake. That meant something, Ross knew...but what?

Jeff had called himself ''Frank McKinney'' when he joined the Paul Reveres and carried all the ID anyone could want to back it up. The agency had planted information to support his cover, though they didn't have a hot line waiting for him, as Belasko's handlers did. Still, Ross thought, it should have been enough. It always had been in the past.

But not this time.

She had no way of knowing what went wrong with Jeff, how they had found him out or what he might have spilled before he died. That he was dead, she had no doubt. Ross

NO RISK, NO OBLIGATION TO BUY... NOW OR EVER!

CASINO JUBILEE
"Scratch 'n Match" Game
Here's how to play:

1. Peel off label from front cover. Place it in space provided at right. With a coin, carefully scratch off the silver box. Then check the claim chart to see what we have for you — FREE BOOKS and a gift — ALL YOURS! ALL FREE!

2. Send back this card and you'll receive hot-off-the-press Gold Eagle books, never before published. These books have a total cover price of $18.50, but they are yours to keep absolutely free.

3. There's no catch. You're under no obligation to buy anything. We charge nothing — ZERO — for your first shipment. And you don't have to make any minimum number of purchases — not even one!

4. The fact is thousands of readers enjoy receiving books by mail from the Gold Eagle Reader Service.™ They like the convenience of home delivery; they like getting the best new novels before they're available in stores... and they think our discount prices are dynamite!

5. We hope that after receiving your free books you'll want to remain a subscriber. But the choice is yours — to continue or cancel, any time at all! So why not take us up on our invitation, with no risk of any kind. You'll be glad you did!

YOURS FREE!

SURPRISE MYSTERY GIFT COULD BE YOURS FREE WHEN YOU PLAY CASINO JUBILEE

©1993 Gold Eagle

CASINO JUBILEE
"Scratch 'n Match" Game

SCRATCH HERE

PLACE LABEL HERE

?

CHECK CLAIM CHART BELOW
FOR YOUR FREE GIFTS!

YES! I have placed my label from the front cover in the space provided above and scratched off the silver box. Please send me all the gifts for which I qualify. I understand that I am under no obligation to purchase any books, as explained on the back and on the opposite page.

164 CIM A7YW (U-M-B-05/97)

Name: _____

Address: _____ Apt.: _____

City: _____ State: _____ Zip: _____

CASINO JUBILEE CLAIM CHART

🍒🍒🍒	**WORTH 4 FREE BOOKS AND A FREE MYSTERY GIFT**	
🍒🔔🍒	**WORTH 4 FREE BOOKS**	
🔔🔔🔔	**WORTH 3 FREE BOOKS**	CLAIM Nº 1528

Offer limited to one per household and not valid to current subscribers.
All orders subject to approval.

had put her grief on hold, made it subservient to her campaign for justice, vengeance—call it what you would.

After eight years with ATF, if you'd asked Ross, she would have said she was immune to shocks, that there was nothing any criminal could do that would surprise her any more. Of course, she hadn't been surprised when Jeff was killed, exactly. Both of them had known that it could happen, working undercover. That was understood. She had been heartbroken and furious, enraged and stricken all at once.

And she had known exactly what she had to do.

The agency had rules and guidelines written down for every situation, from a hangnail to the Second Coming. If you lost a partner in the line of duty, you were automatically removed from active duty on the case in question. There could be no personal involvement in the job, no shadow of a doubt where motives and procedures were concerned. The enemy would kick your ass in court if they could plant a seed of doubt with jurors over one agent's emotional entanglements, a willingness to lie, plant evidence, whatever.

Ginger Ross had seen the writing on the wall that first day, when Jeff missed his scheduled check-in. Once was no big deal on undercover work. An agent couldn't always drop what he or she was doing just to make a phone call. By the fourth missed contact, though, she knew Jeff was in trouble, and she had to call it in.

Which meant that she was finished on the case for good.

But Ross wasn't buying that. No way.

At first she told herself that Jeff might be alive, the Paul Reveres might have him stashed somewhere so they could question him at length. Now, too much time had passed for her to nurse that fantasy along. They would be idiots to hold a federal agent hostage over such a length of time, and whatever else the militiamen might be—fanatics, racists, half-baked revolutionaries—she wouldn't have bet a dime that they were stupid.

Jeff was dead, no doubt about it, and the only problem left for her to solve was what to do about it. Giving up the case wasn't an option. She would rather flush her eight years on the job than loiter on the sidelines while some other team of late arrivals on the scene came in to handle it, treat Jeff as if he was nothing but a name on paper in some dusty file.

Now, there was Mike Belasko to contend with. Never mind his real name; he was trouble with a capital *T*. He had no interest in collaborating with her, even if Ross had felt so inclined.

Which meant that she was on her own. Again. With longer odds against her this time, now that someone could confirm her presence in the area. The agency would have its trackers sniffing after her before another day was out, which only complicated things.

The smart choice would have been to give it up.

"To hell with that," she told the empty motel room that she had rented.

She knew her targets, more or less, and where to find them. All she had to do, from that point on, was to work the details out, decide exactly what to do, how to approach them. There was only one thing she could count on after all.

She would be acting on her own.

"WE KNOW FOR SURE that it was Agent Ross?" Brognola asked.

"Affirmative," Aaron Kurtzman said, speaking on the scrambled line from Stony Man Farm. "We got her voice print off some tapes of interviews conducted by the ATF. It checks."

"Terrific." Brognala's voice sounded as if he had just

discovered piles of feces on his desk. "Where was she calling from again?"

"First time from Taber, Idaho," Kurtzman replied. "Then from Moreland, half an hour down the road."

"The lady plays it safe."

"I'd say."

"And there's no doubt she'd been in touch with Striker." The big Fed's inflection made it seem more like a statement than a question.

"Well, she had his name, the contact number. I'd say it was positive."

"Okay. Keep me advised."

"Will do."

Brognola broke the link and slumped back in his swivel chair, a dark scowl carving furrows in his big, gruff face. The last thing he or Bolan needed at the moment was a complication in their lives—which, based on past performance, meant it was exactly what they should expect.

"Goddammit!"

The one thing Brognola had learned in thirty-something years of working at Justice was that waiting for somebody else to solve your problems was a recipe for personal disaster. In the field that kind of hesitancy got good men and women murdered two or three times every week, at minimum. Promotion to the upper levels of the law-enforcement pyramid reduced the risk of being stabbed, run down by speeding cars or shot, but you still had to watch your back at every turn. Ambition was a killer, and your average civil servant was infected just as easily as any would-be star in Hollywood, New York or Nashville.

Brognola felt relatively safe in his preserve at Justice, but he never really knew when it might blow up in his face. Unlikely as it seemed, the White House might decide tomorrow that the operations run from Stony Man were too extreme—or potentially too embarrassing in an election year—and pull the plug. Congress would never know the difference, since its members didn't have a clue about the program in the first place. If and when that happened, the big Fed would probably be treated to a new assignment, something nice and lame to keep him occupied while he was waiting for retirement, but the others...

What would Bolan do if Stony Man went up in smoke? Brognola had to smile at that, pretending there was any question. Mack would do what he had done before the program started, going back to when he wore his country's uniform in combat or the day he learned about the murders of his family and swore revenge against the Mafia.

Bolan would carry on as he had always done until they put him in the ground. And like Old Blue Eyes, he would do it his way.

Focus, dammit! Brognola chastised himself and dragged his thoughts back to the wilds of Idaho. For just a moment, shifting gears, he wondered what it was about the Pacific Northwest that attracted right-wing fanatics in such concentrations. Ten years ago The Order had begun there, carrying out most of its raids between Seattle and northern California. The Aryan Nations was still based in Idaho, although its strength had faded rapidly in recent years. Skinheads roamed the cities like wolf packs, tormenting any suspected minorities they encountered, and the Paul Revere Militia was only one of several active paramilitary groups in the region. Old Bob Miles, the late grand dragon of the Klan, had once proposed that all "mud people" should be driven from the area to form an all-white nation he had called the Mountain Free State.

It was madness, but the seeds of hate and paranoia seemed to take root much more easily, these days, when trust in government was at an all-time low and John Q. Public needed scapegoats to explain the soaring crime rate, massive deficit, "reverse discrimination" in the workplace and in schools, a steady stream of ethics scandals coming out of Washington and statehouses across the land. You couldn't turn on a television today, without encountering another "statesman" who was caught harassing women, fondling children, taking payoffs, smoking crack or simply breaking campaign promises as if they were made of glass. Eighty-some percent of the American population thought all politicians were thieves and liars, regardless of party affiliations, and the percentage of disaffected citizens was growing all the time.

Why not?

What was there in the news these days to turn the depressing trend around? Executives from the tobacco industry lined up to lie in Congress, claiming they had never found a shred of evidence in fifty years to indicate that nicotine was an addictive drug. If you resisted burglars in your home and injured one of them, you could expect to lose a hefty lawsuit for infringing on the scumbag's civil rights. In prison, homicidal savages had established their constitutional right to free HBO, while filing million-dollar claims against the state because their coffee was too hot, too cold, not decaf—take your pick.

Sometimes, of late, Brognola thought the country was coming apart at the seams...which brought him back to Idaho and Bolan's mission with the Paul Revere Militia.

On his desk a field report from Humboldt County, Nevada, had the earmarks of another outing by the Paul Reveres. He couldn't prove it yet, but Brognola was frankly less concerned with evidence than with the safety of his old friend in the field. He knew full well that infiltration was a very different game from Bolan's normal hit-and-run technique. The marginal uncertainty, his knowledge that some other group of weirdos might be lifting its ideas from Ralph Pike's half-assed novel, made Brognola anxious to confirm his targets prior to taking lethal action.

There had been no letters yet from Winnemucca, but that didn't mean the Paul Reveres were innocent. No one had been killed in Nevada, so it might not qualify in Pike's mind as a Day of the Blade operation. Maybe someone on the team had decided to stop leaving clues, at least on the more mercenary raids, where they were strictly after cash. Then again, maybe the letter was simply delayed or lost in the mail.

Whatever, the big Fed's gut told him it was too much for a mere coincidence. And if the Paul Reveres were raiding now, with Bolan in their camp, then it wouldn't be long before he had the confirmation needed to support a killing strike.

Not long…if he survived.

"Take care," Brognola muttered to himself. "God keep."

RALPH PIKE WAS no stranger to adversity. He had come up the hard way, from a tough neighborhood in St. Louis, "encouraged" to join the U.S. Army as an alternative to jail. It wasn't an auspicious beginning, but once in uniform he had surprised himself. Determination blossomed once he had begun to prove himself, rising through the ranks over time, without the benefit of West Point training or a political guardian angel perched on his shoulder, helping him along. He was a captain when he went to Vietnam, a full-bird colonel when he left, and that alone was testimony to his skill at killing Communists.

It was a skill his country didn't value much these days. The Soviet Union was no more, according to the media, and the Chinese were so busy killing their own people over trifles that they didn't seem to pose much threat to anybody else. Even Pike's old enemies in Vietnam were on their way to favored-nation status, now that they had come up with some more remains of missing U.S. servicemen and started opening their country to American corporations.

It was a New World Order, where money talked and honor walked. Forget about the thousands raped and killed in Bosnia, the hundreds of thousands massacred in sub-

Saharan Africa. Every time he opened the newspaper, Pike was confronted with some new editorial talking about peace in the Middle East, as if the latest round of bombings and assassinations were an aberration rather than the age-old norm.

He understood the East Coast liberals all right, with their desire to sugarcoat the truth or flush it altogether, spreading "politically correct" bullshit in the place of honest discourse. Raise the subject of treason with leaders of either major party, and you might as well be talking to the wall. Mention the threat of Armageddon, and their piggy eyes glazed over. You could almost hear their brains lock up, coherent thought screeching to a halt.

No problem.

There were still enough patriots left in the country to turn things around, if they could just get organized. The Declaration of Independence guaranteed free men the right to armed revolution against oppressive government, and if the time was ever ripe for such a rising, it was now. The signs were everywhere, from urban riots to inflation, teenage pregnancy and welfare, the Satanic holocaust of the abortion clinics—Pike could hardly think about it without grinding his teeth in frustration, bringing on another of the dreaded migraine headaches that had plagued him for the past three years.

He was making a difference now, at least, and when the future texts were written, looking back in sorrow at the 1990s, he would be remembered as a patriot who stood alone at first, then gathered brave men like himself to save the nation of his birth.

To save the country from itself.

The first step had been taken when he wrote *The Lancer Files* and published it himself, selling copies out of his A-frame in Boulder, Colorado, until the book caught on by word of mouth and started selling on its own. Twelfth printing now, and he would have to run off another batch pretty soon. The word was spreading.

More importantly he had survived to see the word made flesh.

The Paul Revere Militia was dismissed by spokesmen for the left-wing media as a bizarre collection of rednecks, gun nuts and neo-Nazis, the kind of people who were prone to eating dirt and marrying their own first cousins. It wasn't uncommon for the "brains" in Washington to call his group subversive, and they were correct in that, assuming that it was subversive to defy a bloated, decadent bureaucracy that served a few at the expense of the majority. Damn politicians with their hands out, federal agents who ignored the Constitution and took pleasure in the violation of a free man's civil rights.

So Pike had seized the moment. Damn right. He couldn't take full credit for himself, of course. One man had never fought or won a war all by himself. It was impossible, in fact. Chris Stone had made a difference, signing on before the Paul Revere Militia had become a household name west of the Rockies, thanks to slander in the media. With Stone and the Reverend Alan Chalmers, Pike had seen his dream become reality—or move in that direction, anyway.

The dream wouldn't be fully realized until he saw a government of free men ruling in America, without the goddamn bureaucrats and humanists who did their best to sabotage most everything the nation stood for. When the time came, some of them—a lot of them—would have to go.

Pike's soldiers had already made a start in that direction, if a meager one. Slowly but surely they were moving toward the glorious Day of the Blade.

He had borrowed the slogan from Hitler's Night of the Long Knives. Granted, Hitler had been a lunatic, with all that stargazing and crap he had indulged in, but you couldn't fault his vision when it came to cleaning up his own backyard. When traitors were identified within the party, Hitler had disposed of them efficiently and ruthlessly. No mercy. Later, when he had a chance to cleanse the world at large, he had been victimized by bad advice. Nonsense about a hollow earth and magic spears, whatever. It had managed to divert *der Führer*'s full attention from the task of killing Communists and Jews.

Pike took exception when the press described him as an anti-Semite. That was leftist bullshit, shoveled by the carload to deceive the public into thinking he was some wild-eyed fanatic on the fringe. In modern America it was taboo to criticize the state of Israel or its agents, even when hard evidence betrayed their sinister, corrupting influence. Same thing with the minorities. If someone pointed out the fact that this or that specific ethnic group was living high on welfare and committing crimes beyond all rational proportion to their numbers in the population, liberals closed ranks to kill the messenger, denouncing him or her as racist, crypto-fascist or some other label calculated to cut off debate on the substantive issues.

Pike had long since given up on mainstream politics. The enemy had grown too fat, burrowed too deep within the body politic for votes to matter anymore. It would take bloodshed, and a good deal of it, to reverse the trend.

In fact the war was under way already, whether Washington acknowledged it or not. The first shots had been fired, and there were more to come. Pike knew he might not live to see the victory, but he had every confidence that patriots would finally prevail.

He would be with his troops in spirit, when they crossed the finish line.

But in the meantime he would have to keep a tight rein on the hotheads in his ranks. The recent shooting, during training exercises, had disturbed him. Pike wasn't prepared to see his vision fall apart because of one or two damn malcontents. If necessary, he would personally mete out justice to the men involved, in such a manner that the rest wouldn't forget his lesson.

It was something to consider while he planned the next moves in his war.

The Day of the Blade was coming.

And for Pike's money, it couldn't arrive soon enough.

APPROACHING POCATELLO from the north on Interstate 15, Stone was watchful, but at ease. The Feds had nothing on him, and the locals didn't even know there was a problem, stupid bastards that they were. If you weren't robbing someone or committing other grievous felonies within their jurisdiction, or if no one put your face on Wanted posters, you didn't exist for the police and sheriff's deputies in rural Idaho.

Which meant the whole damn state.

Stone was a city boy at heart, born in New York and raised beyond age four in greater Los Angeles after his parents split. Ironically his choice of a military career had led him to spend most of his adult life in the back end of nowhere—first training in deserts, mountains and forests, living on Army bases that always seemed to be planted somewhere in the rural South or West; then, after turning mercenary, wandering the Third World in search of wars to fight, becoming more acquainted than he ever cared to be with portions of South America, the Middle East and Africa.

Stone thought it would be stretching things to call Pocatello a city, but a soldier took what he could get. Ostensibly he was on leave from the Reveres, as a reward for work well-done. The colonel would expect him to get drunk, get laid and generally let it all hang out. The possibilities were limited in Pocatello, but a man could find a drink and get his ashes hauled without spending the national debt if he was so inclined.

Chris Stone had something altogether different on his mind.

Subconsciously a part of him was watching out for friends each time he checked the rearview mirror. There was no doubt in his mind that Pike relied on him to keep the troops in line and plan their actions in the field, but the old man wasn't an ignoramus, either. He was as paranoid as hell, believed all that weird shit about the Jews, Communists and "mud people" who sprang from Satan's loins after the six days of Creation. It was all Stone could do to keep from laughing at him sometimes, but he played it cool.

He had a job to do.

The fact that he was good at it didn't mean Pike might not get lucky. If the old man had a nightmare, or he farted twice at breakfast on a Tuesday, he might take it as a sign from God. Once he was plugged into the holy hot line, there was no way to predict what would come next. Stone had been present when Pike scrapped elaborate plans, based on a "feeling" that the operation might be compromised, and twice had seen him single troopers out for no apparent reason, tracking them across the compound with his ice blue eyes.

"That man's an enemy," he would proclaim. "I feel it. Chris, take care of him."

And Stone took care of them, discreetly, with as little fuss and muss as possible. No skin off him if Pike went ape-shit now and then, eliminating some of his own men. It made no difference to Stone at all.

Unless the fickle finger aimed itself at him one day.

He wouldn't know, of course, until it was too late. Somebody else would get the contract, and if the assassin was cool about it, he might take him by surprise. With that in mind, he watched his back inside the compound, and whenever he was off the leash like now.

He passed the Bannock County Fairgrounds on his left and kept on driving toward the heart of town. He had a reservation at a small motel on Hi-Line Road, the Wagon Wheel. It was a hoot how some folks in the West thought everything they built should have a frontier atmosphere around it. Cactus in the flower beds and old lamps on the wall—remodeled to accept electric bulbs, of course— all kinds of rusty farming tools and antique cowboy weapons used as decorations, until you didn't know if you were sleeping in a barn or some kind of museum. Stone would have picked a nicer, slightly more expensive place if it was up to him, but he hadn't been asked to make the choice.

His contact had selected the motel.

One final mirror check before he took the off ramp onto Hi-Line Road. He knew his contact would be waiting for him, on the scene ahead of time. In all the months of their association, Stone had never been the first one to arrive at any given rendezvous. Sometimes he felt like being hours early, just to see the bastard coming for a change, but it was hardly worth the effort. It didn't bother Stone if his contact liked to lead.

As long as he got paid.

The Wagon Wheel Motel was everything he had expected, plus a neon sign out front depicting a huge wagon wheel, part of its rim missing, with a cactus behind it and a bleached-out steer's skull in the foreground.

He had the room number already, knew that it was paid in advance. All Stone had to do was find a parking place and make his way upstairs. When they were done, his contact would take off, and Stone would have the room all to himself for the remainder of his leave. If he felt like it, he could always have a woman sent up later, maybe help him wind down after all that shoptalk.

The stairs were no-slip corrugated steel, constructed with lawsuits in mind. He moved along the second-floor balcony until he reached the door of number 27, paused and knocked.

The door opened immediately to reveal a dark, familiar face.

"How good of you to come," his contact said.

10

Bolan was working out with free weights in the compound's makeshift gym, attempting to relieve some of the tension that accrued from wasted time, when he saw Chris Stone enter, sunlight spilling through the open doorway for a moment, then cut off.

Three days had passed since Stone, Doyle and half a dozen others had returned to brag about their big job in Nevada. There was no official tally on the loot, but Bolan overheard Doyle bragging that they had collected "two, maybe three million" for the cause. Because the radio and television sets in camp were closely monitored, restricted for the most part to a movie channel and the kind of far-right gibberish you find on public-access cable, Bolan couldn't double-check Doyle's boast against the latest media reports.

No matter.

Stone had disappeared again, almost immediately, slipping out on Friday afternoon, returning late on Sunday night. Ostensibly he had gone off on R&R—to lay some pipe. The troops he left behind were jealous, in the way of soldiers everywhere, throughout all time, but the majority regarded Stone with admiration rather than envy.

"You should see him work," Rick Guarini said, on his feet again, his right arm carried in a sling. "The guy's as cool as anything. One time I seen him...well, just take my word for it, that mother can take care of business."

Stone moved toward him now, nodding to others on the way, pausing to share some comment with a guy named Hicks, who had been punishing the heavy bag with bony fists. Hicks nodded in agreement with whatever Stone was saying, and the captain moved along.

"How much you got there?" he asked Bolan, nodding at the barbell the Executioner held, chest high.

"Three-fifty. I'm just warming up."

"Not bad." Stone seemed to mean it. "How'd you like to get your feet wet?"

"Doing what?"

"What difference does it make?" Stone asked.

"Not much."

"Hey, there you go. Be in the mess hall, 1900 hours, sharp."

"Yes, sir."

"I'll see you then."

The Executioner hoped that it would be the break he had been waiting for. The mission had already lasted two or three times longer than usual, and Bolan had begun to feel that he was getting nowhere. Colonel Pike had put him through a crash course in the ideology of the militia movement, with a range of videos and audiocassettes that ranged from the Reverend Alan Chalmers preaching "Armageddon in our time" to more familiar faces from the neo-Nazi movement, spouting their familiar lines about the master race, legal abortion as the "modern Holocaust," Jews dominating the United States from Hollywood to Wall Street. Bolan read *The Lancer Files* and several dozen pamphlets gathered from a list of groups that liked to style themselves as posses, action units and brigades.

Most of it boiled down to a scream of anger and frustration with the modern world, where traditional values had long since gone out with the trash. Blacks and Hispanics didn't know their place. Asians were buying up America, from neighborhood convenience stores to country clubs, casinos, grand hotels and TV networks. Scheming Arabs drove the price of oil up through the roof. Jews poisoned children's minds with filth in theaters, on television, through their music, even as they turned the screws on working men with higher interest rates and taxes, welfare giveaways and foreign aid to Israel.

Bolan could have laughed it off, except that thousands of Americans—no, make that tens of thousands—had already bought the paranoid scenario to some degree. The FBI's most recent count had tallied some 450 right-wing, racist, paramilitary groups at large in the United States, most of them stocking up on arms and ammunition as they waited for the Day. Their weakness, so far, had been competition, ego, call it what you will. Most of them spent as much time bad-mouthing one another as they did the blacks and Jews, but they were dangerous in spite of that. It didn't take a million-man crusade to bomb a synagogue or school bus, to rob a bank or armored car, assassinate a politician or a movie star. The Order, at its peak, had numbered less than thirty active members; the so-called Symbionese Liberation Army had terrorized California for a year, with barely a dozen combatants.

All it really took was a fanatic's dedication and the proper killing tools to do the job. Faith might not move a mountain in the real world, but with dynamite or Semtex, it could come damn close.

He waited until Stone had time to clear the area, then headed for the showers. Nineteen hundred hours gave him forty minutes to get ready for the mission briefing—if, in fact, that's what the gathering turned out to be. Bolan would have to keep his fingers crossed and hope for an assignment that would put him in the thick of things before the job dragged on much longer. Sitting still and waiting for the other shoe to drop had never been his style.

Whatever happened, he would have to get in touch with

Hal Brognola soon, before the big Fed listed him among the missing. It wouldn't be easy, but it could be done.

LOU DOYLE WAS LOOKING forward to another mission. Stone had told him they were breaking in the new man this time, asking whether Doyle had any problem working with a fellow who had kicked his ass. Doyle forced a smile at that and said hell no, he didn't mind at all.

Which was the truth. Not only did he not mind working with Belasko in the field, but Doyle had been counting on it. He had blown his chance to snuff the bastard at the compound, dared not risk a second try so close to home, but going on a raid was something else entirely. Anything could happen once they got out in the field.

Doyle could almost guarantee it.

Details would depend on where they went and what they were supposed to do, of course, but he was smart enough to work the angles any way it played. Belasko being new and all, untested as it were, it would be no surprise if he screwed up his first time out and got himself in Dutch. The way Doyle looked at it, since they had never lost a soldier on a mission yet, the team was overdue.

He spent another minute at the mirror, staring at his taped-up nose, the bruise around his left eye that was changing now from purple to an ugly yellow-green color. He had been no raving beauty to begin with, granted, but Belasko had distinctly messed him up.

And he would have to pay for that. Big time.

Doyle's main regret was that he couldn't take the time to do it properly and make the big man suffer. As it was, he would be forced to make Belasko's death look like an accident, or someone else's doing, to divert suspicion from himself. Stone and the colonel would be looking at him anyway, but Doyle wasn't the kind who felt compelled to spill his guts because somebody started giving him the bad eye. They would have to prove he took out Belasko, and Doyle would split before things went that far.

The Paul Revere Militia had been good to him—no doubt about it, but Lou Doyle wasn't a martyr. Never had been, never would be. In his other life, before joining Pike's private army, he had been an outlaw biker and a hijacker, but he had trouble staying out of jail. Next time they sent him up—in California, anyway—he would be looking at the three-strike rule and life without parole.

Screw that.

He had enlisted with the Paul Reveres because his rudimentary philosophy of life was similar to theirs. Doyle actively despised minorities, though he had never given much thought to the Jews or politics. He faked that part of it at first, until the videos sank in and he began to see what Pike was so pissed off about, with ZOG and all. Once you knew what to look for, hell, the signs were everywhere.

One way to deal with Mike Belasko, Doyle had thought, was to denounce him as a spy, some kind of federal agent sent to infiltrate the compound. That would get him snuffed, all right, if Doyle could make it stick. The only problem was, Stone and the colonel would require some kind of proof now that the whole camp recognized Doyle's grudge against the new boy. And there wasn't any proof, of course. The whole thing would have been a cooked-up crock of shit.

Too bad.

It would have been a high old time to watch him go on trial, knowing his ass was grass before he ever said a word. Doyle could have volunteered to pull the trigger when they finished hearing evidence and brought the verdict in. Plant him back in the woods, as they had done with traitors twice before.

Oh, well.

This way whatever happened to Belasko would be Lou Doyle's little secret. It would cramp his style a little that he couldn't brag about it, but you had to take the bitter with the sweet in life.

And killing Mike Belasko would be sweet indeed.

Doyle checked his watch and saw that it was time to leave for the mess. If he was tardy to the briefing, there was every chance the colonel would get angry and pull him off the roster, fill his place with someone else, and there would go his best shot at revenge.

No, sir. He wasn't letting Belasko off the hook that easily.

Doyle was emerging from his quarters when he saw the new man coming toward him, his long legs eating up the ground. Belasko didn't veer away from him or drop his eyes the way some yellow bastards might have done. One thing about him, Doyle admitted to himself, was that the man had proved that he had guts.

He knew what he had to do if he was going to protect himself. The notion turned Doyle's stomach, but it pleased him, too, made him feel clever, as if he were capable of plotting complicated strategy. He stepped into the new man's path and cleared his throat.

Bolan stopped an arm's length in front of Doyle, and waited for him to make his move.

"You got a minute?"

"Just about," Bolan said. "The briefing's due to start."

"I'm headed over there myself. One thing before we go."

"What's that?"

"I had it coming, what you done the other day." Doyle had to force the words out; they were threatening to gag him. "I was out of line, is what I mean. It looks like we'll be teamin' up here, and I wouldn't want hard feelings in the way, all right? I owe you an apology."

Belasko looked suspicious, but he seemed to swallow it. When Doyle stuck out his hand, the new man clasped it, pumped it twice and let it go.

"Okay," he said.

"We square, then?"

"Far as I'm concerned," Bolan stated.

"Okay, then. Great." Doyle did his best to make his smile look sheepish, almost painfully embarrassed. And he was, in fact, but from the simple act of eating crow.

No problem. In a little while he would be dishing it instead of eating it. And he would watch the new man choke on what he had in mind.

"We'd better get a move on, then," Doyle said.

Bolan nodded, falling into step beside him. Halfway to the briefing hut, they met Jack Cartwright, who gaped at them as if he had seen a ghost. Doyle shouldered past him, making sure the man didn't have a chance to speak and ruin everything.

So far so good.

Somebody once said revenge was better when you ate it cold, something like that. The more Lou Doyle considered that, the more he thought they had it right.

And at the moment he was as cold as ice.

STONE WAITED until everyone was present, ticking off the names and faces in his head. It came as a surprise to see Doyle enter with Belasko, but he told himself his little chat with Doyle had made the difference, keeping him in line. The last thing any of them needed was a feud within the family to screw up any pending operations.

Colonel Pike was seated to his left, against the wall, a watchful presence who, predictably, would take no active part in the mechanics of the briefing. Pike preferred to delegate authority whenever possible, and leave the working details in Stone's hands. Perhaps it made him feel more like a leader, something like a flashback to the days when he was still a player in Vietnam, before his paranoia and contempt for politicians put him on the fast track to retirement from the service.

He was working for a maniac, Stone thought, then caught himself. He didn't work for Pike, no matter what the colonel thought. It was enough for Pike to think he did, while Stone in fact kept working for the man who paid him very well indeed.

So far the covert mission had gone off without a hitch. He meant to keep it that way, see to it that nothing slowed him down, got in his way or ruined his plan. Too much was riding on the line—in terms of cash, his very life itself—for Stone to let his guard down now.

He didn't ask if everyone was present and accounted for. Stone knew the answer to that one already, and he made a point of never letting his subordinates—or his superiors, for that matter—glimpse any attitude that might be taken for uncertainty. He was an expert in his field, and he commanded decent paychecks on the basis of his proved capabilities.

Behind him an altered version of a standard urban street map had been mounted on a corkboard. It had been blown up on a photocopier which sacrificed the nifty colors but left street names and the labels on specific landmarks legible.

"We're after something special this time," Stone began. "It's an opportunity for us to test our urban combat skills, give ZOG a swift kick where it hurts the most and fatten up our war chest for some future actions. This mission won't be easy, mind you, but it's possible. Sometimes you have to gamble if you want a decent payoff in the end."

There were no questions from the floor, but he hadn't expected any. Stone had taught these men to speak when they were spoken to, or hold their doubts in check until free queries were invited.

Stone took a folding pointer from his pocket, opened it with a flick of his wrist and tapped a point dead center on the blownup city map.

"The U.S. Mint in Denver, Colorado," he announced,

indicating a rectangle that had been red on the original map, reproduced by the photocopier in a faded tone of gray. A deathly silence followed Stone's identification of the target.

"Now a straight run at the mint is suicide," he added, letting them partway off the hook when he felt that the tension had been strung out long enough. "We haven't got the manpower to execute a mission that complex. Not yet. But we can make a score on this, regardless, and come out ahead."

Still nothing from his captive audience. All eyes were locked on Stone, the map forgotten as they waited for him to explain what they had to do.

"We can't get in," he said, "but cash still comes and goes. New money flows out to the banks, old money comes to the incinerator. Some of it gets moved in helicopters, but the bulk goes overland in armored trucks."

He had them now, could almost feel the room relax. Some of them had been in on the Ukiah job, and all of them except Belasko knew about the robbery. They had the confidence to handle armored vehicles.

"We're looking at the old stuff coming in," Stone said, continuing. "The new bills have sequential numbers. Even if we fenced them, we'd be luck to get twenty-five cents on the dollar, with the heat a job like this will generate. Old bills, they've been around, picked up some wear and tear, but we can spend them right away, no sweat."

A couple of his soldiers smiled, imagining the trucks packed with dirty, rumpled, faded currency, all destined for oblivion. It was entirely logical for a guerrilla army to liberate some of that cash and use it against the tyrannical state.

"The guards are T-men," Stone continued. "Treasury. Not Secret Service, but the next best thing. They're trained and armed with automatic weapons—Uzis, M-16s, some riot shotguns, semiauto side arms—but they've never had to use them off the range. Your average stickup men don't rob the mint. It's like Fort Knox. You just don't try it.''

Several of his troopers frowned as the happy visions in their minds turned into blood and gun smoke, bodies sprawled on blacktop, sirens, flashing lights.

Stone dropped the other shoe. ''And that's their weakness,'' he declared. ''They've got contingencies mapped out on paper, all rehearsed and memorized, but no one's ever had to use them. When a hundred years or so goes by without a challenge, people let their guard down. They don't mean to, they're not even conscious of it, but it happens all the same. It doesn't matter if we're talking bank guards, or that old Maytag repairman on TV. There's a margin of error even when they feel alert. Reaction times slow down, corners get cut, the team gets sloppy.''

Stone had their full attention, something between awe and fear. He could almost hear their taut nerves humming in the silence as he finished speaking. These men would be idiots if they weren't concerned about the prospect of facing down armed Treasury agents in broad daylight, but concern—even a touch of old-fashioned fear—could help keep soldiers on their toes. The problem came when caution turned to cowardice, and troops were paralyzed.

No problem there, Stone thought. With one exception, these men had already proved themselves in action, fighting for the cause.

Time to proceed.

''All right,'' he said, and turned back toward the map. ''Here's what we do.''

THEY LEFT AT DAWN, twelve men in four vehicles, rolling south on Interstate 15 through Pocatello, Inkom, Malad City, Woodruff, into Utah. In Salt Lake City they divided forces, two cars following the southern route to Provo, where they picked up Highway 6 and stuck with it until it intersected U.S. 70, eastbound, crossing the Colorado border near Grand Junction. The remainder of the team drove north and east on U.S. 80 from the Utah capital, across southern Wyoming to Cheyenne, and south from there on U.S. 25 to Denver. It took time, but Stone had minimized their risk of being picked up on the highway. They would stay in separate motels and rendezvous next morning, at a preselected coffee shop in Wheat Ridge, taking it from there.

Stone's plan was slick enough to work. Not foolproof— there was no such thing—but still a solid piece of strategy. Bolan couldn't prevent the heist from going down unless he threw his cover out the window and attacked, when Stone and company were least expecting it. In that event he had a chance of taking out the hit team, but there were no guarantees. Assuming he survived, his penetration of the Paul Revere Militia would be finished; there could be no going back. He would be left without the handle he was seeking on their contacts in the outside world, their friends in government—aside from young Neal Martz.

In essence it would mean that he had wasted precious time, when he could just as easily have blitzed Pike's rural compound on day one.

His other options were to let the raid proceed and play an active part, thus jeopardizing lawmen and civilians, or to somehow tip off Brognola before the strike went down. The latter course had built-in perils of its own, but Bolan reckoned he would have to try, then take the consequences if he failed.

It would be complicated by the fact that he was riding with Chris Stone. The third man in their car was Jerry Schaefer, stocky but well muscled, five foot ten, with blond hair thinning on top. He smoked unfiltered Camels and appeared to live in mirrored shades.

Somehow the Executioner would have to lose both of them for the time it took to call Brognola's office, and in such a way that neither would suspect what he had done.

He got his chance in Elgin, Utah, when they stopped for gas and truck-stop burgers. Sitting at the counter, Bolan waited until they were served, then told the others that he had to take a bladder break. Schaefer ignored him, but it seemed to Bolan that a small frown weighted down the corners of Stone's mouth.

He walked back through the diner, through a narrow passageway with neon-painted arrows pointing Bolan toward the rest rooms labeled Gals and Gents. The doors opened to the Executioner's right and left, with a wall-mounted telephone between them.

Bolan glanced behind him, making sure that he was out of sight from where his two companions sat, then lifted the receiver, thumbed a coin into the slot and waited for the dial tone's hum to fill his ear. He tapped out eleven digits and turned to face the dingy corridor, the dining room beyond.

It was a toll-free line, unlisted, with the number changed at monthly intervals and known to fewer than a score of individuals. The voice that answered on the second ring was a recording, no one Bolan recognized, informing him that he had sixty seconds from the tone in which to leave his message.

Thinking swiftly, Bolan stuck to basics. Date and place—he didn't know the time or the specific route as yet—along with bare-bones details of the plan. No more than thirty seconds into it, he saw a shadow fall across the far end of the corridor and cradled the receiver, shouldered through the door marked Gents and made a beeline for the nearest urinal.

The rest-room door had barely closed behind him, its pneumatic shock absorber seeming to take forever, when it hissed open again to admit Chris Stone.

"Must be contagious," the militia captain said.

"Could be," Bolan replied, zipping up his fly and tugging on the handle that unleashed a miniwaterfall. He moved to wash his hands, watching Stone's back in the mirror set above the row of sinks.

The captain had his head down when he spoke again, as if the question were directed to his genitals. "You up for this?" he asked.

"I'm here," Bolan said, wondering if the suspicion in Stone's voice came from his own imagination. No, he told himself, this guy survived on paranoia.

"Some guys think they've got it covered," Stone replied, "but when the time comes, they just fall apart."

"No sweat. I carry my own weight."

"I thought so, but it never hurts to ask, know what I mean?"

"Sure thing."

"We've done all right so far," Stone said as he reached up to flush his urinal. "No problems that we couldn't handle in the field. Three guys looked like ringers at the compound. I was only sure on one of them, but what the hell. It's better safe than sorry, right?"

"I've always thought so," Bolan answered.

"What I mean to say is that we don't let anybody jeopardize the team."

"Makes sense."

"Housecleaning is a bitch sometimes, but we take care of business."

There was no way to avoid the warning in Stone's words. It wouldn't qualify as any kind of overt threat, but Bolan got the message, loud and clear.

"If you need somebody taken care of," he replied, "just let me know."

Stone frowned at him again, then shook his head as he was lathering his hands. "Not yet," he said. "With any luck it won't be necessary."

Bolan shrugged. "Whatever. I'm just heading back before the food gets cold."

"Be right behind you," Stone replied.

And the Executioner had a feeling he could take that to the bank—or to the mint, in this case.

If his luck went sour, he could take it to his grave.

11

The details of the plan were relatively simple. Pike and
Stone had somehow found out that the truck they wanted
would be rolling into Denver from the south, on U.S. Highway 25, with its arrival at the mint scheduled for
10:30 a.m. on Wednesday. They would stop it on the road
near a suburban settlement called Dream House Acres.

Even with a dozen men and four cars, though, the
scheme involved no small amount of risk. There would be
four guards, minimum, inside the armored car, and it wasn't
unheard-of for the Treasury Department to dispatch an extra watchdog team on certain shipments, sometimes without
informing the regular crew. It was a combination of security
and quality control that could double the guns covering any
given shipment, without advance warning.

Bolan knew better than to ask how Stone and company
had marked the cash truck in the first place. That was for
Brognola to discover, if and when he had the time. Just
now, as he sat waiting for the armored car to show, Bolan
was more concerned with whether the big Fed had picked
up on his message and been able to decide which routes to
cover.

If he failed, there would be bloody hell to pay.

Their Chevy Blazer was parked on Arapahoe Road, near
the on ramp for Highway 25. They wouldn't see the truck
approaching, but Lou Doyle was spotting for them, staked
out on the shoulder of the highway with his flashers on,

one of his friends tinkering beneath the open hood. As soon as Doyle had visual contact with the target, he would radio ahead and put the other teams in motion, bringing up the rear as others moved to head it off. Before the T-men got to Belleview Road, they should be in a box.

From that point onward, it could still go either way. Stone's team was packing all the hardware necessary to complete the mission, including two LAW rocket launchers, a Barrett semiauto .50-caliber rifle, Colt Commando and MGP-84 Mini submachine guns, plus individual side arms, frag grenades and tear-gas canisters. Bolan carried a Beretta Model 92 in shoulder leather, with one of the Mini SMGs, but it would be tough going against eleven men with similar or larger weapons, even if he somehow took the first few by surprise.

The mechanics of the hit were basic: try to head off the armored vehicle and blast it with LAW rockets before the driver could swerve around their roadblock or plow through it, crushing anybody in his way. They couldn't fire the rockets in a drive-by manner, since the back-flash would have roasted other passengers or set the gunner's vehicle on fire. Once they had stopped the truck—if they did stop it—then the race was on to crack it without burning up the cash inside, grab all the money they could carry and head out of there before police arrived.

It might have been a trifle easier to hit the target on a smaller street—while it was idling at a stoplight, for example—but that would have placed them closer to the mint, somewhere in downtown Denver, with police and Feds more apt to execute a swift response. This way, at least in theory, fewer witnesses would have a telephone available, and any cops who took the call would have to scramble to the outer limits of their jurisdiction.

Hardly perfect, but it was the best Stone could have managed in the circumstances, and the shock would guarantee some banner headlines if they pulled it off.

Or if they didn't.

Bolan had thought about his part in the proceedings, trying to decide how far he could go without breaking his own private rule against shooting a cop. If they had been dispatched to raid a syndicate delivery service or a rival group of neo-fascists, Bolan would have waded in without compunction, but the targets would be lawmen this time. He wasn't prepared to kill or wound them to protect his cover, but his problem was already more complex than that. Suppose he faked it, pulled his shots deliberately and missed each time, but someone else on Stone's team did the killing. Would he not be equally involved, for watching it go down, when he could have devised a way to intervene?

How far was he prepared to go?

The tinny sound of Lou Doyle's voice cut through his brooding thoughts.

"Heads up!" he said. "Let's everybody roll."

STONE DOUBLE-CHECKED the safety on his Colt Commando, holding it across his lap as Jerry Schaefer fired up the Blazer's engine and stood on the accelerator. Moments later they were pulling onto Highway 25 and merging with the traffic there.

"I see it!" Schaefer blurted, leaning forward in his seat and pointing with his pug nose, like some kind of hunting dog. Perhaps a hundred yards ahead of them, the armored car was running in the center lane, without a problem in the world. The small, smoked-glass windows made it physically impossible to tell if any of the guards was checking out their back-trail, but it stood to reason that they would be. There was nothing else to do on a run like this if they weren't checking out the route for enemies.

Doyle was behind them, hopefully gaining by now, but Stone could see one of the other vehicles, a Toyota Land Cruiser, already passing the target and nosing ahead. The

Ford Explorer should be up there, too, screened from his line of vision by the armored car.

They had chosen larger vehicles with off-road capabilities in case anything went wrong. Stone had no illusions about being able to block the armored car with two normal passenger vehicles, not if it was hurtling down the highway in a race with death. That's why the point cars had LAW rockets at the ready, to complete the box, while Doyle's team had the Barrett .50-caliber bringing up the rear.

Stone felt the thrill of incipient action, starting as a pleasurable tightness in his groin, then spreading to his limbs until he almost had a weightless feeling. He had to control himself at times like this, keep the heady sensation from running away with him, sweeping him into rash behavior and stupid mistakes. It could happen, he knew from experience. And if it happened now, well, he could wind up dead.

Stone checked the outside mirror on his door and caught a glimpse of Doyle's team, closing up in the Isuzu Rodeo. Not bad for rolling from a standing start, but Stone would have demanded no less.

Any moment now...

He saw the brown Toyota start to make its move. A careless drift, it looked like, if you didn't know the plan. Drivers were like that, edging over lane markers with casual negligence, no signal to warn the drivers behind them. Two lanes over, invisible to Stone with their target in the way, the Ford Explorer would be doing likewise, only drifting in the opposite direction toward the Toyota, boxing in the armored car before its driver knew exactly what was happening.

They had enough lead that it wouldn't be alarming to the enemy for several seconds yet. The driver of the armored car might even be amused, with a potential fender-bender going down in front of him. He wouldn't stop to help or offer testimony, though; that kind of chivalry was strictly banned, since anything that happened on his route could be the bait for an intended trap.

No, he would cruise by, assuming that he had the chance.

The point cars were some eighty yards in front when both slammed on their brakes and nosed in toward the center lane. It wasn't much of a roadblock, with four lanes to cover, but time was more important than bulk.

"Do it!" Stone told Schaefer, but the Blazer was already moving in to block the armored car's retreat.

And to Belasko, riding in the back he said, "Be ready, now!"

It all came down to timing. If Hicks and Barnhill got their first shots off without a hitch, they had it made—the first part of the operation, anyway. If one or both of them screwed up and missed the mark...

Stone didn't want to think about it, couldn't think about it now, with tension like a strong hand clamped around his throat and threatening to strangle him. He swallowed hard, willing himself to relax as the first LAW rocket was launched downrange.

A hit!

He saw the armored car veer sharply, dark smoke pouring from the point of impact at its nose. The second blast felt like an echo of the first, and told him both rounds had gone in on target.

Perfect.

He had warned his rocketeers against trying to take out the driver directly, not from any great concern for human life, but rather out of fear that superheated fragments entering the passenger compartment might contribute to destruction of the loot. Stone hadn't come this far to see the money accidentally burned up by one of his own team.

The armored car was swerving, skidding, trailing sparks—the left front wheel was gone—and grating to a halt. A few more seconds, and they would be right on top of it.

Stone gripped his submachine gun, getting ready to go EVA.

"Heads up!" he told the others. "Time to rock and roll!"

DOYLE SAW THE BLAZER'S brake lights flare, more traffic hurrying to pass on either side before the drivers scoped out what was happening. At least it wasn't rush hour, with thousands of cars on the highway, jammed bumper to bumper.

Bad enough as it was, Doyle thought, but they could handle it.

And he could handle Mike Belasko, too.

One shot, in the confusion, ought to do the trick. If there was shooting from the truck, so much the better, but Doyle had come prepared, in any case. His backup side arm was a Ruger Mark II Standard semiautomatic with the barrel stripped and drilled, a homemade silencer in place. Ten rounds of .22 long rifle ammunition gave him all the chances he would need to take Belasko down without a fuss, and he could always ditch the piece before Stone got around to searching members of the team.

It was as close to foolproof as a plan of Doyle's had ever been, or ever would be. After nearly blowing it back at the compound, he had taken time to think the problem through, and he was ready.

Drifting smoke and flashing brake lights told him it was coming down. He checked out the vehicle's dashboard clock and saw that they were thirty seconds off. The armored truck was running late, but not enough to matter. Thirty seconds, give or take—to hell with it.

What was half a minute among mortal enemies?

Doyle saw the Blazer braking, poked his driver in the ribs. "Catch up, there!" he demanded.

"Right!" No argument from Eddie Cole. He had his

eyes fixed on the target and the intervening traffic, looking for an opening.

When Cole started to brake, Doyle was ready, with the Colt Commando's safety off, a quick touch underneath his jacket to be sure the Ruger was in place. He had already bungled one attempt on Belasko's life, couldn't afford to miss again, but he was also on a mission, facing federal agents, and if Doyle forgot that crucial fact, there was a fair chance that his next ride would be in a hearse.

The truck slid to a stop, and Doyle bailed out, crouching behind his open door for cover. A backward glance showed him other cars braking or swerving to avoid impact, drivers gaping through their windshields at the scene before them. It was something like an action movie, but without the lights and cameras, the technicians hanging out around the sidelines. No blanks in the guns this time. Whoever took a hit on this set would be staying down.

And Lou Doyle meant to guarantee that one of those who did was Mike Belasko.

Stupid bastard, thinking Doyle was weak enough to try to patch things up with an apology, instead of getting even for the pain and the humiliation he had suffered at Belasko's hands. That kind of thinking proved he was a weakling, underneath the show of martial skill and muscles. Anyone who couldn't hold a grudge was no damn good at all, in Lou Doyle's way of thinking.

Up ahead the armored truck was stopped now. Someone would be on the radio or reaching for it, bent on calling out for help. For all Doyle knew, the truck might even come equipped with a dead-man's alarm, beaming out a signal to the cops or Feds if no one in the vehicle was capable of taking action on his own. Whatever, there was bound to be some lag time yet before the cavalry arrived. They didn't need a lot of room, as long as everything went down like clockwork, as per Chris Stone's plan.

Well, almost everything.

Doyle craned his neck to peer across two empty lanes, and saw Belasko standing upright at the rear end of the Blazer, ski mask covering his face, his carbine pointed at the back doors of the armored vehicle. Doyle had a clear shot at the man, but he couldn't risk it yet. He needed some confusion, something to distract Stone and the others from Belasko's plight before he made his move.

And he would have it, any second now.

Stone had his bullhorn out, a compact model with all the volume of a full-size one. You could hear inside an armored car. It wasn't loud, but they would hear what Stone was saying, if they hadn't all been deafened by the rockets going off.

In fact it hardly mattered either way. If there was no response from those inside the truck in ten or fifteen seconds, it would be the signal to proceed and crack the target by aggressive means. No sweat.

And when the shooting started, Doyle would have his chance at Belasko.

He was smiling at the prospect, reaching back inside his windbreaker to triple-check the Ruger, when he heard the sound of helicopter rotors overhead. Not close yet, but approaching rapidly.

A scowl etched Doyle's face, beneath his mask, as he turned toward the sound and peered up at the azure sky.

BOLAN WAS COUNTING down the microseconds, wondering if there had been some kind of hitch at Brognola's end, when he heard the chopper coming from behind him. Pivoting and glancing up, he recognized the Bell 206 LongRanger, painted black, with U.S. Treasury emblazoned on the fuselage. He knew the helicopter seated seven, but there would be more guns coming overland.

Suddenly a dozen things began to happen all at once. There was another blast from the direction of the armored car—grenade or rocket, Bolan couldn't say for certain—

and a couple of the cars that had been passing to his left collided, grinding metal, screeching rubber as they jostled to a halt. Above him, someone in the Bell LongRanger switched the whirlybird's loud hailer on and started blaring orders at the hit team.

"Lay your weapons down and raise your hands above your heads! You are surrounded by federal agents! Lay down your weapons *now!*"

"Surrounded, shit!" Schaefer barked, turning from the armored car and raising his Colt carbine toward the sky. "Surround this, you dumb bastards!"

Bolan was flashing on his own next move, still weighing options, when a bullet struck the tinted window near his face and left a clean hole in the glass. He heard no shot, but ducked instinctively, guessing the direction that the shot had come from, scuttling for cover at the rear of the Blazer. There had been no shot that he was conscious of, but what did that mean?

Doyle?

A glance toward the Isuzu showed him nothing. Doyle was nowhere visible, his two companions on their feet and trying to decide if they should keep on covering the armored truck or bring the helicopter under fire.

Gunfire stuttered from the far side of the armored truck, and someone in the growing traffic pileup in the northbound lanes was leaning on his horn. Some others picked it up, until the sounds of shooting and the vision of the helicopter finally cut through their irritation at the slowdown. By the time they laid off on the beeping, southbound sirens could be heard, approaching from Denver.

More shots, sounding like a submachine gun, and then Schaefer squeezed off a burst from his Colt Commando toward the chopper. In the time it took to register his action, someone in the whirlybird was firing back. It sounded like an M-60 machine gun, bullets knocking divots in the pavement, flaking paint in perfect, shiny circles from the Blazer's roof as they punched through.

There was nothing Bolan could do in the circumstances except to keep his head down. He was just another masked, armed robber to these federal agents and the cops who were hell-bent on blocking off the crime scene. Brognola might have advised them that he had a man inside the hit team, but the lawmen would have no way of identifying him—nor would they care that much once they came under fire.

In moments they would be surrounded. Edging out from cover, hugging one side of the Blazer as he edged toward Stone's position, Bolan had to watch for bullets coming from both sides. The first round hadn't come from a police gun—he was sure of that—and while he had a fair idea of who had pulled the trigger, there was no time to debate the question or to dish out payback at the moment.

Stone was crouched beside the Blazer, cursing bitterly as Bolan reached him. In frustration he squeezed off a short burst at the target vehicle, his bullets rattling harmlessly off armor plate. He almost jumped when Bolan laid a firm hand on his shoulder, drawing his attention from the armored car.

"The cops'll be here any time," Bolan said.

"Shit! Goddammit!"

"We can make a stand right here or live to fight another day. Your call."

Stone seemed to ponder the decision for a moment, glancing back and forth from the disabled target to the helicopter spiraling above their heads. The racing sirens had already halved their distance, drawing closer by the heartbeat. As he hesitated, yet another burst of automatic fire sprayed from the Bell LongRanger, catching one of Doyle's men and spinning him around before he went down like a rag doll on the pavement.

"Let's get out of here!" Stone said.

"Good call."

As Bolan crouch-walked toward the Blazer's open door,

Stone started shouting through his bullhorn at the other Paul Revere commandos. "Fall back! Scrub the mission! That's an order, people!"

Bolan threw himself across the Blazer's back seat, staying low, and heard the front doors slam almost in unison. The engine roared to life, and Schaefer dropped the four-wheel-drive into reverse, tires smoking as he stomped down on the gas.

STONE COULDN'T BELIEVE what was happening. The plan had been refined to near perfection, always granting that you couldn't tell when some dumb farm boy in a squad car would attempt to spoil the fun. They had allowed for that contingency, but choppers in the air and instantly converging sirens were a very different ball game. They bespoke coordination, and he knew damn well that even if the men inside the target vehicle had managed to broadcast a coherent alarm in the available time, there was no way on God's earth the Feds or locals could have mounted a response like that in seconds flat.

"We've been set up!" he said to no one in particular.

"Say what?" Schaefer was half-turned in his seat, with one hand on the steering wheel, the other braced against the Blazer's padded console as he made tracks in reverse.

"Somebody set us up, goddammit!"

"I don't get it."

Even as he spoke, Schaefer was stepping on the brake pedal and cranking the wheel to his right, putting the Blazer through a wild one-eighty that left crescent skid marks on the pavement. They were facing head-on toward the north-bound traffic now, pointed the wrong way, but it didn't seem to bother Schaefer as he stood on the accelerator and their vehicle leaped forward, engine roaring underneath the hood.

Stone gave up trying to explain and glanced back through the tinted windows at his soldiers, scrambling to evacuate the scene of their abortive strike. The Blazer's roof was pocked with half a dozen bullet holes, light streaming through them in pencil-thin shafts that reminded him of spotlights in the distance, beacons for some Hollywood premiere. There was another hole, too, in the tinted window on his side, back toward the rear, which had apparently come from a different angle, but he put it out of mind, no time to ponder the phenomenon.

There was a good chance that all of them would be killed or captured sometime in the next ten minutes. In his mind Stone had already shifted from offensive to defensive mode, his full attention focused on the act of breaking through the ambush, getting out of there before the noose drew tight around his neck.

They had discussed the possibility of an aborted mission, followed by a scramble to escape, and while no one expected to be ambushed at the scene, all the same principles applied. They were supposed to scatter, leave the interstate and take their chances on the smaller streets and back roads if they could, fleeing in all directions of the compass, to divide their adversaries and reduce the number of assailants any three-man team would have to face. Doyle had lost one man already, but Stone couldn't waste time grieving over someone he had barely known by sight. All of his troopers carried false ID, and even if the lawmen got a make on fingerprints, there would be nothing to connect the dead man with his fellows in the Paul Revere Militia.

They were clean that way, but they were also still in deep, deep trouble.

Stone didn't plan for it to end like this. He wouldn't spend his life in prison under any circumstances. It was better to die fighting, if it came to that, and take as many of the bastards with him as he could...but better still to wriggle through the net and make his getaway, to live and to enjoy the paychecks he had been accumulating in a Cayman Islands bank since he began his latest mission.

They were weaving in and out through traffic, most of it stalled with the jam up ahead, startled drivers gaping at the Blazer as it raced in the wrong direction, plunging against the tide. Another backward glance showed that the helicopter hadn't followed them, but had remained to hover fifty feet above the wounded target vehicle.

The chopper jockey had no way of knowing which car held the leader of the team, which one he should pursue to nab the brains behind the operation. At the moment, Stone knew, someone in the whirlybird would be in contact with their reinforcements on the ground, directing squad cars, SWAT teams, whatever was in the area.

Somebody would pay for this ambush, if Stone survived to sort it out and fit the puzzle pieces into place. Someone had sold him out, and there was only one fit punishment for treason. Stone would cap the bastard personally when he found out who it was.

But first he had to save himself.

He saw an on ramp coming up, a semitrailer grumbling toward the far lane of the interstate, northbound. "Take this one!" he commanded, rocking in his seat as Schaefer spun the wheel and passed the eighteen-wheeler with perhaps an inch to spare on Stone's side of the Blazer.

THE HOMES in Dream House Acres hardly lived up to their name, but Bolan wasn't interested in the architecture at the moment. He could still hear sirens from the interstate, and part of him expected the Bell LongRanger to strike at any moment, skimming low across the housetops with its big M-60 blasting, riddling the Blazer and the men inside.

It would be no work spotting their vehicle from the air, with bright, new bullet scars across the roof. And once they had been spotted, closing in to make the kill should pose no challenge to a pilot or a gunner with experience.

He was so busy looking for the chopper that the squad car took him by surprise. It had been running with its siren off, lights flashing, but the shrill note started wailing as the black-and-white fell in behind them, coming from a side street, closing the gap with power left to spare.

"What are you waiting for?" Stone shouted. "Take them out!"

It could be death to hesitate, he realized, but Bolan had to buy some time. He reached behind the backrest of his seat and found the latch that let him lower it, converting half the passenger compartment into cargo space. That done, he crawled back toward the tailgate with his Colt Commando, knowing he would have to take some action in the next few seconds or his cover would be blown.

The wheelman made his mind up for him, reaching underneath the dash and yanking on a lever that released the tinted tailgate window, raising it on lifts like miniature shock absorbers. Bolan had a clear shot at the squad car now, with nothing to prevent his laying down a screen of cover fire. As if to prove his point, the squad car's shotgun rider chose that moment to unload three shots in rapid fire, his right arm out the window, braced against his outside mirror. One slug hit the Blazer's tailgate, while the other two went wide.

No time to hesitate. Bolan sighted down the carbine's barrel, aiming at the cruiser's grille. Despite the hype that showed up every now and then in firearms magazines, he knew it was improbable in the extreme that 5.56 mm rounds would penetrate the squad car's engine block. As for the danger posed by ricochets, he compensated, aiming low, an inch or two above the tail car's bumper.

Now!

He milked a 3-round burst out of the Colt Commando, followed by another. One round struck the bumper with a clang that Bolan heard above the siren's wailing, but the rest went home, tore through the radiator, launching jets of steam. The cruiser was already swerving when his last rounds ripped into the front tire on the driver's side and finished it.

He saw the black-and-white veer sharply toward the curb, sheer off a mailbox bolted to the sidewalk there, and plunge nose first into a hedge of sculpted juniper. The Blazer vaulted forward, swung around a corner on two wheels, and the pursuit car with its shaken occupants was lost to view.

"All right!" Jerry Schaefer crowed at the wheel.

Beside him Stone was scowling as he snapped, "Shut up and drive!"

12

Whoever named the Roadhouse, Ginger Ross decided, either lacked imagination or was hooked on Patrick Swayze films. In either case the combination restaurant and night-club was exactly what she would have looked for in a juke joint outside Blackfoot, Idaho.

Most of the vehicles out front were pickup trucks or four-wheel-drive vehicles, with half a dozen motorcycles for variety. Smoke wafted out to meet her as she crossed the threshold, and the music blasting at her as she stepped inside was hard-core country-western.

She had been watching Ralph Pike long enough to know that this was where he came when he felt like relaxing, letting down what little hair he had. He made the drive to Blackfoot two or three times a month, if he was in the mood. She had bribed a twenty-something barmaid to alert her when he showed his face the next time, and the call had come that evening, just an hour earlier.

Ross had dressed in record time, and still looked good enough to give the locals whiplash as she made her way in the direction of the bar. Her dress was short and tight, low cut for ample cleavage, basic black. High heels showed off her legs to good advantage, and she put a little something extra in her walk, determined not to pass unnoticed in the crowd.

Pike had a booth off to one side, his usual, where she had seen him more than once. The other times, she had dressed down and taken pains to be ignored, unlike tonight. This time she found a bar stool in the colonel's line of sight, where she could hit him with a profile, and she made a point of staring at him, long enough to catch his eye, before she turned away and ordered a drink from the bartender.

The first man to approach her was a six-foot-something cowboy in a Stetson and a tailored Western shirt. His heavy paunch was resting on a belt buckle at least six inches in diameter, inlaid with gold and several flashy stones. Ross suppressed an urge to giggle.

"Mind if I join you, ma'am?" the cowboy asked.

"I'm waiting for my date," she replied.

"Must be a damn fool to leave you on your own this way, if you'll excuse my sayin' so."

"I'll take that as a compliment."

"That's the way it was intended, ma'am." He hesitated, clinging to his beer with one hand, while the other worked its way into a pocket of his too-tight jeans. "Maybe I could keep you company, just while you're waitin'."

"That's a bad idea," she said, sipping her whiskey. "He's the jealous type if you get my drift."

"Well..."

"Really, no. No, thank you."

"Okay. Maybe another time."

"You never know."

The cowboy moved away, and Ross turned back toward the mirror set behind the bar. She picked out the reflection of Pike's booth, and found the colonel on his feet. Too late, for Christ's sake! He was calling it a night already, and she hadn't even had a chance to—

Wait.

Instead of heading for the door, Pike moved in her direction, sidestepping a pair of tipsy dancers. Another moment, and the colonel was beside her, flagging down the barkeep.

"I'm impressed," Pike said.

"Excuse me?"

"With the way you handled Wyatt Earp just now."

"Oh, yes?"

"Economy and style are admirable qualities." Pike nodded toward her drink and added, "May I?"

"I just started this one."

"No problem. We've got time...that is, unless you plan on chasing me away."

She forced a cautious smile. "I haven't made my mind up yet."

"That's fair," he said. "Perhaps you'd join me at my table while you weigh your options."

"I don't know."

"No strings attached," Pike said. "I never force myself on women."

"Never?" she asked, teasing him.

"I can't afford to," Pike replied. "At my age, most of them can clean my clock."

"I doubt that very much," she told him, thinking, if she had half a chance, she'd *stop* his clock.

"Appearances can be deceiving," he informed her.

"So I've heard."

"Then, shall we?"

Ross made a point of thinking for another moment, finally nodding. "Well, okay. But only for a little while."

"Of course."

Halfway to the colonel's booth, the cowboy intercepted them. He had a mean look on his face, and no beer in his hand this time.

"So, this your date?" he asked.

"Is there a problem?" Pike inquired.

"There just might be. I don't much care for being made to play the fool."

"You ought to take that up with Mother Nature, son. There's nothing I can do to help you."

Ross weighed the odds. The cowboy was several inches

taller than her quarry, and he outweighed Pike by seventy or eighty pounds. Still, there was something in the crew-cut soldier's bearing that compelled his enemy to hesitate.

"You making fun of me?" the cowboy asked, as if unable to believe his ears.

"Would I do that?" Pike asked, eyes twinkling.

"You just might, if you were sick and tired of livin'."

"Let's assume I am," the colonel said. "What would you do about it?"

"I might have to kick your sorry ass," the cowboy answered.

"Be my guest."

The big man gaped at Pike for several seconds, then drew back his right hand for a roundhouse swing. Anyone could have ducked that punch, the way he telegraphed it, and the colonel had a shark's smile on his face as he stood waiting for it to arrive.

At the last second, when the fist was hurtling toward his nose, its owner totally committed and off balance, Pike stepped toward the cowboy, underneath his swing, and hooked a punch into his abdomen, the stiffened fingers of his right hand disappearing into flab.

The cowboy doubled over, gasping, and his last few beers came back to haunt him in a spewing rush. Pike dodged the spray and brought a bony elbow down behind the Stetson, impacting where the cowboy's skull and spine were joined. His adversary went down in a boneless sprawl, without a sound, and didn't move again.

"Is he all right?" Ross asked.

"He'll survive," Pike told her, "but he won't enjoy it for the next few days."

"I guess that proves you lied to me," she said.

"How so?"

"About those women whipping you, and all."

"I've never hit a woman in my life," he said without a smile.

"Can I believe that?"

"I devoutly wish you would."

"You know," she said, "this smoke and noise is getting on my nerves."

"Perhaps we should go somewhere else."

"You wouldn't have someplace in mind, by any chance?"

"I might," the colonel said. "I just might have at that."

IT COULD BE WORSE, Brognola told himself, then wondered how.

A solid week with no word from the Executioner, then he got this cryptic call about a raid directed at a shipment heading for the U.S. Mint in Denver. The big Fed had pulled some strings and mobilized a warm reception for the would-be bandits, knowing even as he did so that he might be signing Bolan's death warrant.

That part of it had worked out well enough. There was no sign of Bolan at the scene, no indication that he had been wounded in the shoot-out. As it happened, only one man from the team of something like a dozen had been left behind—a body you could read through when the whirlybird's machine gunner got through with him. The ID in his pocket, a Montana driver's license, was professional quality but strictly bogus, no use at all in their effort to find out who he was.

As if it mattered.

Brognola already knew the Paul Revere Militia was behind the Denver strike, for all the good it did him. Bolan was his living proof, the one man who could never testify in court. If they identified the shooter from the crime scene, even linked him up to the Reveres, it still proved nothing from a legal point of view. Militia leaders would reply, and rightly so, that they couldn't control each of their members every waking hour of the day. You didn't prosecute the Boy Scouts or the Jaycees, for example, if one member got in trouble with the law. Before you took that step, you needed evidence of a conspiracy to wrap the package up.

So far, so bad.

At least one other member of the raiding party had been wounded by authorities. Brognola knew that much from bloodstains found in an abandoned vehicle, dropped off in Boulder when the fugitives picked up another stolen car. From the amount of blood, it could have been a fatal wound, but no more bodies had been found as yet, and the big Fed wasn't about to hold his breath. There had been ample time to dig a shallow grave—or drive back into Idaho, for that matter. Without a warrant, which required some damn persuasive paperwork behind it, Brognola would never get permission to go looking for a fugitive among the Paul Reveres.

Besides, whatever move he made in that direction only heightened Bolan's risk, the jeopardy he faced while he was dwelling in a hostile camp.

The Justice man felt like pacing, but he knew the nervous energy would better be directed into thinking through his problem. Bolan had appeared, however briefly, to touch base, then he had dropped back out of sight. The Denver raid had come down right on schedule, but the money had been saved this time. He was assuming Bolan had been on the raid, but even that couldn't be positively verified.

It came as no surprise to Brognola that Bolan hadn't checked in with the Stony team since Denver. He was working on a cover, after all, and living in an isolated compound, probably with access to a telephone restricted by the brass in charge. On top of that, the paranoia harbored by your average militia member would be cranked up with the Paul Reveres to something like hysteria, after their close encounter in the Mile-High City.

"What a mess!"

Brognola didn't realize that he had spoken until he heard the sound of his own voice and nearly jumped out of his seat. What was it Dan Quayle said that time, when he was mixing up his slogans?

It's a terrible thing when you lose your mind.

The big Fed wasn't ready for a ticket to the laughing academy yet, but some days he felt like it, wading hip deep through the bullshit they shoveled in Washington, pretending that it smelled like roses. He had long since given up on any kind of meaningful reform in Wonderland, content to do his job in peace when bureaucrats allowed him to. The red tape didn't slow him down as much as some, because the covert nature of his operation kept the normal headhunters and number-crunchers at a distance, but he had to please the White House all the same, and you could never really tell what was inclined to please a President from day to day.

It might not please the Man, for instance, if he knew that Brognola's best operative in the field was living with the same right-wing guerrillas who had tried to heist twelve million dollars on its way to the incinerator. Never mind that the attempt had failed, that Brognola had dealt the Paul Reveres their first defeat since they declared war against ZOG. The President was still a politician, first and foremost. Any problem he encountered would be automatically assessed in terms of gains or losses at the ballot box, aside from any impact on America, her citizens or national defense.

Domestic terrorism gave a black eye to the President on more than one account. For openers he was the nation's Chief Executive, bound by oath to see the laws enforced and to defend the Constitution from attack by foreign enemies or hostile native sons. Additionally, when the violence seemed to spring from—or, at least, to feed on—rhetoric espoused by members of the opposition party, it was difficult for any lifelong politician to resist the game of pointing fingers, fixing blame. That kind of play could backfire if it seemed the Man was using tragedy to his political advantage, using corpses as his stepladder to win a second term, or maybe pushing legislation on the hill that would apparently revise key features of the Bill of Rights.

The backlash was inevitable, in a case like that, and it could strike on several different levels simultaneously. On one hand it gave the opposition party tons of ammunition for the next campaign, painting the Man as simply one more politician, more concerned with job security for number one than with the seeming meltdown of American society. Meanwhile, at the grass-roots level, where frustration turned to bitterness and festered into violence, repressive measures only won more recruits for the lunatic fringe.

Conversely if the President said nothing, he was "soft on crime," a "wimp" who let himself be pushed around, vacillating on critical issues while John Q. Public lived in daily fear of violence on the streets.

All things considered, Brognola was glad that he had never run for office. With his luck he might have won, and where would he be then? Better to work behind the scenes, he thought, and know the satisfaction of a real accomplishment from time to time than to be plodding on a treadmill in the public eye.

Brognola brought his mind back to the problem of the Paul Revere Militia, wondering where Bolan was this night, if he was safe. A quiet DNA analysis would tell them whether it was his blood spilled in the abandoned holdup vehicle, but the odds were eleven to one against a positive match, and the Executioner had survived far greater odds than that.

Whatever those results, however, the big Fed already knew the answer to his other question. Bolan was not safe, by any means. He had infiltrated a viper's nest, with nothing but his wits to keep him breathing, and there was no guarantee that he would make it out alive.

"Hang tough," Brognola told the empty office, not surprised to hear his voice this time. And once again, for emphasis, "Hang tough, big guy."

THE WHOLE WAY BACK to Idaho, Lou Doyle was fuming. They had missed the payroll, he had blown his shot at Belasko and the Feds had wasted Billy Kravitz right before his very eyes, as though they were shooting stray dogs from the air. It didn't help at all to know that he and Hicks had wriggled through the net, unscathed, to make their getaway. The Denver raid had been a failure any way you looked at it, and someone had to pay when things went wrong.

It was a law of nature, as immutable as gravity. Each failure had its built-in consequences. They were inescapable. It made no difference whether you were talking humans or amoebas when a predatory action fell apart. In nature, if a hunter failed to make a kill, he didn't eat. Mankind had modified the rules a bit, inventing systems of reward and punishment to modify behavior, but it all boiled down to consequence.

For every fuckup, someone had to take the heat.

The lawmen had been waiting for them back in Denver. That was obvious to anyone with eyes and half a brain, which meant Doyle had worked it out before they reached the Colorado line. The mint got three or four shipments minimum each day, with more trucks headed out to banks and such. No way the Feds trailed each and every shipment with a helicopter, or had all those squad cars standing by. No way at all.

Which meant that someone must have leaked the plan. There was a traitor in the ranks somewhere, but who? The colonel and Chris Stone had put the scheme together, briefed their team and sent the raiders on their way, with Stone in charge. In simple terms that meant a minimum of thirteen men—unlucky number—had been privy to the plan. Allowing for the fact that some of those may have informed a barracks buddy at the compound, and the bud-

dies may have spread the word around, it was impossible
for Doyle to guess how many men—even their wives and
kids, perhaps—knew some or all of what the raiders meant
to do in Colorado.

You talk about security, and all the time you might as
well be sending copies of your battle plan out to the *New
York Times.*

It wasn't his job to discover who had leaked the plan, or
how, but Doyle was thinking he could turn the circum-
stance to his advantage if he played his cards right. When
the brass began to look for suspects, infiltrators, it was only
natural that they would look at new men first. That put
Belasko squarely on the spot and made Doyle think that
maybe something positive *did* come out of disaster, after
all.

His task would be to help Stone and the colonel cultivate
the notion that the new boy on their team had let them
down. Not merely dropped the ball in combat, but deliberately sold them to the Feds. Belasko would deny the
charge, of course, so Doyle would need some kind of evidence, something that he could plant—a seed of doubt, no
less, that would sprout thorns and crucify his hated enemy.

He had the long drive back to think about what he should
do. They ditched the wheels the Feds had seen in Littleton
and stole another car, dropped it at Orchard Mesa, near
Grand Junction, and were well across the border in their
third car of the day before Doyle let himself relax. He had
worn gloves in the Isuzu, and in all the other stolen cars,
so he wasn't concerned about the risk of being traced
through fingerprints. Doyle wouldn't make it that easy for
ZOG to hunt him down.

He thought about Kravitz again, but only in passing. On
field operations it came down to the quick and the dead,
with some dumb luck thrown in to keep the game intriguing. Kravitz always claimed he had no record, either criminal or military, so it should be difficult for anyone to make

a firm ID, and if they found out who the poor dumb bastard was, so what?

The militia was already under surveillance, like a dozen similar groups nationwide. The Feds had planted one man in the ranks already. Doyle knew that because he had been present at the bastard's trial and helped to plant him when the sentence had been carried out. Connecting Billy Kravitz to the noise in Denver might increase the heat a little, but the Feds would still be short on their precious probable cause.

Doyle wasn't a legal scholar, but he knew enough to get by in a pinch, no pun intended. He was more or less conversant with the law regarding warrants, searches and the like, as it was applicable to his own nefarious activities. Since joining the militia, he had also spent some time with Colonel Pike's collection of books on constitutional law. He had absorbed some of the theory by osmosis, trying principally to concentrate on practical applications that would help his ass stay out of jail.

Right now, though, he was focused on revenge.

Denver made it three times that Belasko had embarrassed him, and that was three too many for Lou Doyle to tolerate. Payback was long since overdue, and he was anxious to get on with it, by one means or another.

He would have to think about it, make sure that he didn't screw things up a fourth and final time. Belasko would be doubly jumpy after the near-miss in Denver, brooding on it, even if he didn't blame Doyle. It could be tricky, planting evidence to make him look like one of Uncle Sammy's boys—much easier to simply rub him out, Doyle thought—but there were ways to pull it off. It would require a little thought, perhaps some help.

Jack Cartwright would oblige, if for no other reason than that he was scared of Doyle. With reason, too. He understood Doyle's violent streak better than most, realized that the man was capable of almost anything when he was riled.

At some point pure rage kicked in with a vengeance, and rational thought went out the window, for all intents and purposes.

At such times Doyle could even scare himself.

But not this night.

He felt clear headed, cool and confident. It was the kind of mind-set he required to formulate a plan and see it through, to nail Belasko's ass once and for all.

The bastard had been lucky so far, but his luck was running out. Another day or two at the outside, and Doyle told himself the new boy would be history.

The prospect kept him smiling as he crossed the border into Idaho and headed back to camp.

PIKE'S HOME away from home was a two-bedroom A-frame on the outskirts of Blackfoot, set back from Highway 39 a hundred yards or so, along a dirt-and-gravel track. His two-year-old Jeep Cherokee made short work of the hill, and Ginger Ross was painfully aware of being isolated as they pulled into the bare dirt turnaround that passed for Pike's front yard.

"You're off the beaten track up here," she said as Pike switched off his lights and killed the engine.

"That's the way I like it," he replied. A moment later he was opening her door and bowing slightly as he offered her his hand. "My lady."

Ross watched him to make sure he wasn't mocking her. As far as she could tell, she hadn't dropped a stitch so far, nothing to put the colonel on his guard. It had been his approach, his conquest, if you like, and she could think of nothing that would lead him to suspect her. All the same, she drew great reassurance from the Colt Mustang .380 automatic in her purse.

She hadn't hesitated when the colonel asked her to accompany him, and there would be no hesitation now. She owed it to her partner to go the limit in pursuit of those who killed him. It would be a simple matter, once they got inside the A-frame, to produce her pistol, press it to the colonel's crew-cut skull and finish him.

But that wouldn't be good enough. Pike's death would leave the others unaccounted for, at large, unpunished for their crimes. She needed evidence enough to blow the whole damn operation, shut it down for good and guarantee its active members some substantial prison time. There was no doubt in Ross's mind that they possessed and dealt in outlawed weapons, that they were responsible for several robberies and murders. All she had to do was prove it in a court of law.

Anything she did from this point on could jeopardize her final case. It was a risk she took, in getting closer to the colonel, but some risks were unavoidable. Her testimony might be compromised, if things got out of hand, but she was counting on the kind of solid evidence—weapons and documents, at least—that would be capable of standing on its own at trial.

In case she didn't live that long.

The A-frame's furnishings were on the Spartan side, apparently selected to enhance the owner's image as a rugged, no-frills kind of man. Or maybe, she decided, Pike just didn't give a damn.

The walls were hung with photographs that traced Pike's years in military service, from his boot-camp days to Vietnam and afterward. There was an eight-by-ten of Pike and General Westmoreland shaking hands. Another of him with a senator who had gone on to run for President, without success. She didn't recognize the other faces in those photographs, but made a show of staring at them anyway.

"Bushmills, I do believe," Pike said, and handed her a glass of whiskey.

"I'm impressed. Again."

"My ears are still in decent shape," he said. "Everything works, in fact."

"I wouldn't be surprised."

"Why did you come with me tonight?" he asked.

"Why wouldn't I?" she countered with a teasing smile.

"The age difference, for one thing." Pike examined her with narrowed eyes, as if he were about to guess her weight. "You can't be more than thirty-one or thirty-two."

"What difference does it make?"

"To me? Not one iota. I'm just curious, is all."

"You're an impressive man," she said. "The way you took care of that cowboy…"

"That windbag?" Pike dismissed his recent adversary with a smile. "He wouldn't last five minutes on a decent training course, much less in combat."

"So, you were a soldier." Glancing toward the wall of photographs for emphasis.

"I *am* a soldier," Pike corrected her. "You never really leave it. Once the job gets in your blood, you're hooked."

"You mean, you're still on active duty?"

"That's a story for another time," Pike said. "Right now I feel like making love, not war."

"Why, Ralph," she said, smiling demurely, still the tease, "whatever do you mean?"

Pike took her hand and led her toward the stairs that served the open loft above their heads.

"Come on with me," he said, "and I'll explain it to you, step by step."

13

The camp was quiet as the sun went down the day after their raid in Denver. There had been a small memorial for Billy Kravitz and Paul Fletcher who had been wounded in the getaway from Denver and had bled to death before his teammates swapped their vehicle for cooler wheels. Instead of leaving him behind, Jack Cartwright and his driver had put Fletcher in the new car's trunk and started watching for a place where they could plant him, safe from prying eyes.

The Paul Reveres were mourning, in their own strange way, with the Reverend Alan Chalmers turning up for the memorial. Instead of speaking to forgiveness and the afterlife, however, Chalmers reeled off battle texts from the Old Testament, in which Jehovah—Yahweh to the Paul Reveres—commanded that his people seize the land of Canaan from its first inhabitants by killing every man, woman and child among them. That should be a warning to the enemies of the militia, Chalmers railed; they should consider that before they put another gallant patriot in prison or dispatched him to an early grave. Bolan kept waiting for some mention of the fact that the dead "soldiers" had been killed while trying to commit armed robbery, but Chalmers managed to avoid that fact, if he was even conscious of it.

Whatever doubts the Executioner had on that score were banished half an hour later, when a court of inquiry convened with Pike and Chalmers on the panel. Stone was first to testify, then the survivors of the team were called in, one by one, to give their version of events. At Bolan's grilling, Pike asked all the questions, while Chalmers and two sergeants picked at random sat and glared at him, as if expecting him to break down and confess some wrongdoing.

The questions were routine: had anything unusual occurred between the time he left the compound with his team and their arrival at the target zone in Denver? Had he noticed any other member of the team behaving strangely? Talking on the telephone? Exchanging signals with a stranger at their rest stops on the highway? Bolan answered negatively straight across the board, suspecting he had caught a break by being on the team with "Captain" Stone. He volunteered a story of the near-miss shooting, for the hell of it, and watched them puzzle over that before he was excused.

Good luck.

The final verdict was announced near sundown. Pike summoned the surviving members of the holdup party to his quarters. They stood in ranks of three, Stone off to one side by himself, while Pike announced his findings. Chalmers had already left the compound.

"The evidence is clear that someone set us up," the colonel said without preamble. "Someone, somehow, tipped our enemies about the raid. There is no other explanation for the swift response. As for the traitor's actual identity—" Pike glowered at them, spread his callused hands "—we just can't tell right now. That may curtail our operations for a bit, but I *will* solve this problem. You can rest assured of that. And for our Judas, when he's been identified, my justice will be swift and sure. You may wish to consider that, in case one of you has some information he forgot to share before the court of inquiry. I will be making further inquiries, with other methods, in the next few days. Dismissed!"

Doyle was lighting up a cigarette as Bolan left the colonel's bungalow. "I've never seen the old man that pissed off before," Doyle said.

"Are you surprised?"

"No. Hell, we've had our ringers in the bunch before. The Feds and locals send them in from time to time. We root them out, though."

"Sounds like one slipped through the net."

"You never know." Doyle shrugged. "We'll get him, though."

"What was that business about 'other methods'?" Bolan asked.

"Oh, that." Doyle took a long drag on his cigarette and blew the smoke out through his nostrils. "Colonel Pike, he's got a friend in Coeur d'Alene who's like some kind of private eye or something. Runs a lie-detector business, too, for companies that want to catch their cashiers stealing money, shit like that. A couple times before, they brought him down to run some tests, you know. It helps cut through the bullshit."

Bolan felt a hard knot forming in his gut. The polygraph was not infallible, and he knew it could be beaten with the proper frame of mind. A hard-core psychopath could beat the so-called lie detector seven, maybe eight times out of ten, because he simply had no conscience to react when he was under pressure. Otherwise, the annals of police work were replete with cases where the wrong man flunked a test and had been branded as deceptive on the basis of a medical condition or a nervous twitch, perhaps a simple glitch in the machine itself. One classic text maintained that polygraphs, administered by experts, were inaccurate at least one-quarter of the time.

Which would mean nothing whatsoever if they wired him to the box and started grilling him about his loyalty to the Paul Reveres. He had no drugs or hypnoimplants to assist him with that kind of questioning, and there would be no realistic chance of fighting his way out once he was hooked up to the polygraph, disarmed, the evidence of treason scrawled in ink for Pike and Stone and everyone to see.

Before that happened, Bolan knew that he would either have to flee the camp or find another suspect to divert the inquisition from himself. Someone who would surprise the brass, embarrass them enough that they would give up on the search for other infiltrators in the camp.

But who?

He glanced at Doyle. "I'm going for some coffee. Want some?"

Doyle considered it, then shook his head. "No, thanks. You go ahead. I got the second watch tonight. I'd better catch some winks."

"Okay, I'll see you later."

"Yeah," Doyle said. "I wouldn't be surprised."

THE PLAN WAS hardly perfect, but it was the best Lou Doyle could do on such short notice. It had helped when Belasko started asking him about the polygraph, a little nudge in the direction he should take to polish off his scheme. The new man hadn't sounded nervous, but he damn sure would when Doyle relayed the story to Chris Stone and Colonel Pike. By that time he would have the script revised and edited, Belasko sweating through his damn fatigues, he was so spooked by the idea of sitting for a lie-detector test.

Of course, he needed more than that. A whole lot more. For all he knew, Belasko might sail through the polygraph with flying colors. There was nothing to suggest that he would fail, in fact, since Doyle was cooking up the whole damn thing himself out of thin air.

No matter.

By the time he finished scamming, there would be no reason for the test at all...and that was good for Doyle, since there were certain things he didn't want to answer for himself.

It wasn't much, okay, but he had pulled a couple holdups

on his own during the past few months, when he was on furlough from the compound. A fat little convenience store in Rexburg was the first, and then a liquor store in Burley. Nothing major, and he hadn't harmed a soul, but he was seven thousand dollars to the good.

Doyle kept the money in his footlocker, because inspections of the barracks didn't go that far, the colonel feeling that his soldiers needed some degree of privacy. It wasn't what you'd call a fortune, but it was enough, perhaps, to substitute for thirty pieces of silver when he fingered Belasko as their live-in Judas.

If the plan was going to work, however, he would have to plant the money on Belasko—and come up with a story that would sell the colonel on his own reliability, while making sure the new boy took a fall.

Belasko had been helpful, when he asked about the polygraph. Doyle might have had some trouble otherwise, but he could see it now. They'd come out of their meeting with the old man, and Belasko's looking worried, asking what the colonel meant when he said "other methods" would be used to single out the traitor. Doyle had talked to him about the polygraph examiner from Coeur d'Alene, and poor old Mike had seemed right jumpy when he heard the news. All factual so far, except the part about Belasko's mood—and when Doyle thought about it for a while, damned if he didn't start believing that the new boy *had* been jumpy. Hell, it could be true, at that!

The rest of it was easy. Doyle had been concerned at seeing how Belasko took the news. He started thinking over how their trouble started when Belasko joined the team—first trouble in the compound, Rick Guarini being shot and all, then the snafu in Colorado. If there was another, older traitor in the camp, it stood to reason they would have been taking losses earlier. Back in Ukiah, for example, maybe even when they went to smoke that big-mouthed Jew in Billings.

Right. So, Doyle was curious about Belasko, and he trailed the new boy to his quarters, sneaky like, to see what he could see. And what he *saw,* in fact, was old Mike hiding one hellacious wad of greenbacks in his footlocker, beneath his mattress—Doyle could work out the details when he had found a place to stash the cash. It struck him funny that Belasko would be carrying that kind of bankroll, and that he would feel the need to hide it from his fellow Paul Reveres. The only incidents of theft in camp, since Doyle had been there, had involved some of the little kids with sticky fingers, and their mamas whipped that out of them right quick.

That was his story, then, and he would stick to it. He had no choice, as a loyal soldier of the counterrevolution, but to tell the colonel and Stone what he had seen. Of course, he hoped Belasko would be cleared, since they had patched up all their troubles and become good friends before the Denver raid...but if his new pal *was* a traitor, well, the movement took priority over the individual.

Belasko might respond by telling Colonel Pike the truth—that he had never seen the money before—but it would come off sounding lame, like some kid getting caught with chocolate on his face when there's a cake gone missing from the kitchen. What? Who, me?

Forget it. He was toast.

Now all Doyle had to do was fetch the money from his own footlocker, plant it on the new boy, wait a little bit and spill his guts to Stone. It would be more in keeping with his character and military protocol if he didn't approach the colonel with his tale. Anyhow, he reckoned Stone would be most anxious for the traitor to be named, since he was taking heat himself for the snafu in Denver. They could sell the case together, Stone believing it was true, while Doyle took his shot at an Oscar-winning performance.

Lighting another cigarette, Doyle smiled to himself and

started to walk toward his barracks on the far side of the
compound. In another hour, give or take, he would be done
with Mike Belasko, and Belasko would be on his way to
hell. It would be worth the seven grand to see him squirm.

And watch him die.

BOLAN TOOK HIS TIME heading back to his quarters, spending half an hour in the mess hall, over coffee, and thinking
about the dilemma he would face if Pike called in his expert
on the polygraph. No matter how he turned the problem
upside down or inside out, the only real solution he could
think of was to flee the camp before the PI put in an
appearance.

Dammit!

In effect his flight would mean the past ten days had
been a waste, aside from Bolan's role in scuttling the Denver raid. He would be forced to start from scratch, with
Pike and company on full alert once he bailed out.

No matter. When he came for them next time, he
wouldn't need an invitation, and they wouldn't know that
he was in the neighborhood until it was too late.

Things happened in a soldier's life, and there was no
point crying over circumstances he couldn't control. A strategic withdrawal was not the same thing as running away
from a mission. Bolan would be back to see the Paul Reveres, and soon, but he couldn't afford to let himself be
trapped inside the compound with no ready means of
escape.

If he was going, Bolan told himself, he might as well
get on with it. For all he knew, Pike's friend from Coeur
d'Alene could be en route that very moment, bearing the
Executioner's fate in his hands.

He finished his coffee, then took the mug back to the
counter where it would be washed. The sun was down when
Bolan left the mess hall, cool darkness settled over the compound, with minimal lighting on display. The first round of

nocturnal sentries would be at their posts, but he had no doubt of his ability to pass them unobserved. If necessary, he could always take one out and leave the corpse for someone else to find.

It would be better, though, if he could slip out unopposed, cause no one to suspect a problem in the camp before the following day's breakfast call, when he would fail to put in an appearance. As it was, he would be forced to leave his wheels behind and walk the six or seven miles to Taber—no great challenge, if he wasn't being hunted, but a major problem if he had a pack of well-armed vigilantes on his heels.

In terms of hardware, he could stop off at his vehicle before he left and pick up the Beretta. Just in case. Before he did that, though, he felt like changing into warmer clothes. That meant a quick stop at his quarters, where, with any luck, he would be spared long-winded conversations with his bunk mates. Maybe tell them he was headed to the showers, thus explaining why he took a change of clothes out of his footlocker.

No sweat.

Survival mode was kicking in as he approached his quarters, soft light showing through the windows there. He came up quietly, surprised to see the door ajar, but thinking little of it. Someone passing in or out had left the door that way by accident. So what?

A scuffling sound froze Bolan on the threshold, one hand on the doorknob. What was that? Not feet, exactly. No, it sounded more like someone riffling through the contents of a drawer or chest, removing items or replacing them. One of the men who shared his quarters, probably, retrieving something from a footlocker.

No problem.

Bolan stuck his head inside the door and froze again.

Lou Doyle was rummaging around inside *his* locker, as if searching it. For what? It hardly mattered, knowing that he had nothing of an incriminating nature to be found. Bolan hadn't been fooled by Doyle's gesture of friendship on the night before the Denver raid, so he wasn't surprised by what he saw.

Two choices came to mind. He could confront the man and see what came of it, or he could slip away without the clothes and leave right now, while Doyle was occupied. He was about to flip a mental coin and trust the outcome when he saw Doyle reach into a pocket and withdraw a roll of greenbacks, held together with a rubber band.

And just like that, the choice was made.

"Is that for me?" Bolan asked, stepping in to close the door behind him.

Doyle's head whipped around, a sudden grimace on his face as if he'd hurt himself. The prowler struggled to his feet, glanced briefly at the money in his hand, as if deciding how to play it out.

"It's yours, all right," Doyle said at last. "Your money from the Feds for selling out the Denver operation."

"Makes me wonder why you had it in your pocket," Bolan said.

"You think the colonel will believe that, asshole?"

"Let's find out."

It was a bluff, but Bolan didn't think Doyle would call. His hatred for the new man on the team had been established early on, and it was poorly camouflaged by his display of camaraderie the past few days. There would be questions if they went to Pike together. Doyle might crumble under questioning, forget to keep his story straight.

The wheels were turning in Doyle's mind as he returned the money to his pocket, putting on a sneer. "It's better if I see the colonel by myself," he said.

"That isn't how it works."

"It will be," Doyle responded, "when you're dead."

He drew a switchblade from his pocket, snapped it open with a practiced gesture, dropping to a combat crouch as he advanced on Bolan, circling slowly to his adversary's left. Unarmed, the Executioner prepared to defend himself with empty hands, conscious of his adversary's direction and determined not to let him reach the door.

Both men were clear on one point now. The best way to present their different stories was without a living tongue to contradict a given version of events.

Doyle's first move was a feint—a short jab with his knife hand, instantly withdrawn, while he kept circling toward the barracks door. Bolan surprised him that time, moving in the opposite direction, clockwise, to prevent his getting any closer to the exit. Blocked, Doyle muttered something that was almost certainly a curse, and froze just long enough to calculate his next move off the jump.

Another feint, if you could call it that. Doyle took a kind of hopping step off to his left, and seemed to swing his empty hand at Bolan in a roundhouse strike, then lunged straight forward with the switchblade toward his adversary's stomach. It hadn't required much thought—but, then again, Doyle hadn't had much time.

Bolan was waiting for the thrust, deflected it, caught Doyle's wrist in his left hand and swung underneath it, as if they were partners in a 1950s dance contest. The move extended Doyle's arm to the limit, with his elbow locked, and Bolan brought his free hand slashing down against the joint with force enough to break it.

Doyle cried out in pain and dropped his knife. That could have been the end of it, but Bolan didn't feel like arguing with the man in front of a tribunal where the members had been hanging out with Doyle for months on end, and the Executioner was an unknown quantity.

Instead, he wrenched the broken arm up higher, higher, putting Doyle on tiptoes, straining to relieve the agony, his head thrown back, teeth clenched around a scream that would erupt in seconds flat. The knife-edged hand that crushed his larynx seemed to come from nowhere, smashing into Doyle's throat with destructive force.

He staggered, clutching at himself with one hand, while the other dangled uselessly. His face was beet red, going purple, as he lost his balance and went down on his knees. Eyes bulging, tongue protruding from between his bluish lips, Doyle fought to draw a breath, but all in vain.

A tracheotomy might still have saved him, but it wasn't in the cards. Bolan stood back and let the numbers run until his would-be killer toppled forward, slack and sprawling on the floor. His prostrate body shivered once, twice and lay still.

The first part of his hasty plan had gone without a hitch. Part two would take some salesmanship, but Doyle had set the stage. One open footlocker, contents in disarray. A wad of cash in Doyle's left trouser pocket. Switchblade open on the floor, a few feet from his corpse.

Touch nothing, Bolan thought, in case they had a way of checking fingerprints.

In fact, he didn't need to dress the stage. It all came down to explanations now, convincing Pike and Stone that Doyle had tried to set him up. Beyond that, it would be a short leap to the ultimate conclusion that Lou Doyle had been their traitor all along.

He hoped so, anyway.

No time to think about it now, though, with the body cooling even as he stood there.

Bolan turned away from Doyle and went to find the sergeant of the guard.

"So, LET ME SEE if I can get this straight," Pike said. "You come back from the mess hall, where you're having coffee, and you find Doyle in your footlocker."

"Kneeling beside it, yes, sir. He was going through my things, such as they are." Bolan was careful not to fake contrition as he spoke. He was supposed to be the injured party here, with nothing to feel sorry for.

"And then you asked what he was doing," Stone suggested.

"No, sir. It startled me, I guess, to see him there. I was about to call out, when he took this roll of money from his pocket and began to put it in my locker."

"Then what happened?" the colonel asked.

They were in Pike's quarters, Bolan seated in a folding metal chair before the colonel's desk, Pike facing him. Chris Stone roamed the smallish room at will, hands clasped behind his back. It all reminded Bolan of an old flick where they give some guy the third degree, but nobody had touched him...yet.

"That's when I asked him what the fu— I mean, what he was doing, sir."

"And what did he say?" Pike inquired.

"Nothing, at first. He got up off his knees and put the money back into his pocket."

On the desk in front of Pike, the roll of bills had been fanned out, revealing several thousand dollars in C-notes and fifty-dollar bills. Doyle's open switchblade served the colonel as a paperweight, holding down the greenbacks.

"Go on," Stone prodded.

"Well, let's see...he stood up, put the money in his pocket and he said, 'It's payback time.' Something like that."

"Payback for what?" Pike asked.

"His nose, I guess." The shrug was almost casual. "He acted like I was supposed to know."

"Okay. What happened then?"

"It struck me as odd," the Executioner replied. "I mean, he sounded pissed, but he was putting money in my locker, so I asked again what was he doing."

"And?"

"He laughed at me, and said the old man—beg your

pardon, sir—the old man was about to find his traitor. Said he'd tried to smoke me twice himself, but I was lucky. Now he'd let the old man handle it.''

Pike glanced at Stone and frowned. Bolan couldn't see Stone's reaction, and he dared not turn around to check.

"What did you say?" the captain asked from somewhere behind him.

"I told him let's go see the old—I mean, the colonel, then. Both tell our stories, right up front. That's when he went ballistic on me, pulled the knife. You know the rest.''

"Not quite," Pike said. "Doyle had the only weapon in the room?''

"As far as I could tell, yes, sir.''

"But he's the one who wound up dead," Stone said.

"Well," Bolan said, shrugging again, unable to resist a smile, "he wasn't all that fast.''

"I gather not. That thing he said about the traitor, when you saw him with the cash. Did he make any reference to the Denver operation?''

"Not directly, sir. But when he said he'd tried to kill me twice, I took it that the Denver shooting was the second time—after Guarini in the woods last week.''

"You've had a lucky break," Stone said.

"I guess that all depends, sir.''

"Say again?''

Bolan knew he was pushing it, but something needed to be said. If he appeared complacent in the face of violent death—a death that he had caused—it might convince the brass that *he* had staged the scene instead of Doyle.

"I mean," he said, "it all depends on what you finally believe. Doyle was a friend of yours—well, anyway, a member of the group—before I ever came along. Most people, give them half a chance to choose between a friend's lie and the truth some stranger tells them, they'll go with the friendly bullshit nine times out of ten.''

"This is a military court, son," Pike informed him, "not

some old maid's coffee klatch. We're looking at the evidence, and that will be the only basis for our ultimate decision. Understood?''

"Yes, sir."

"All right. Dismissed."

It was approaching midnight as he left the colonel's quarters, few lights burning in the compound. Stay or go? he asked himself. Would they be watching him? Did he have time to slip away?

Forget it.

He had drawn his hand, and he would play it through.

But on the way back to his quarters, Bolan stopped off at his vehicle and picked up the Beretta.

Just in case.

14

Three showers didn't do the trick, but Ginger Ross knew she couldn't spend her whole life scrubbing places where the old man's mouth and hands had touched her. She felt raw in spots already, and she still had work to do.

Besides, the strongest soap available would never touch her soul.

The night with Pike had been a total blunder, from the legal point of view. If she was called to testify against Ralph Pike in court, his lawyers would be tickled pink. Trot out the smut and paint her as a woman scorned, or claim entrapment at the very least. She could imagine what the press would say: "A whole new trend in 'undercover' work," something like that. The media would hang her out to dry, and rightly so.

What she had done with Pike crossed every line she could imagine, shattered every rule that she had ever heard of in her eight years on the job. Her testimony, much less any evidence she gathered after bedding down with Pike, wouldn't only be compromised, but it would be thrown out in a heartbeat. The colonel wouldn't need a Johnnie Cochran to defend *that* case. A first-year law student with grades below the norm could get it tossed out in his sleep.

So, why did she do it, then? she asked herself as she was getting dressed to leave her motel room.

And came up with the same, predictable reply: because the bastards murdered Jeff.

It wouldn't wash with her superiors, of course. In fact, that kind of thinking was the very reason they had tried to pull her off the case when Jeff went missing. She was too involved from that point on, not thinking clearly, acting like a woman rather than a trained professional.

Screw that!

With Jeff dead, there would be no case. Whatever evidence he had collected on the Paul Revere Militia had to have vanished with him. If they found his body someday, buried in a shallow grave a hundred or a thousand miles away from Pike's headquarters, it would only prove what they already knew: that he was dead. Ballistics might identify the gun that killed him, if they found the weapon, but she wouldn't hold her breath on that one, either. Pike and his militiamen might be fanatics, rednecks—call them what you would—but no one ever said they were a pack of idiots.

Too bad.

She could have used some really stupid adversaries at the moment, to offset her own stupidity. The worst thing was suspecting that her night with Pike would turn out to be wasted time, with nothing real to show for it except the way she felt about herself.

They called them pigs and whores, she thought. Maybe they were right, in her case, anyway.

She caught herself before that train of thought could run its course. Her partner had not just been manhandled or screwed; he had been killed. That was the bottom line, and anything that she could do to even up the score, no matter how humiliating to herself, Ross was ready to proceed.

In fact she had gained one thing from the long, disgusting night with Pike: a glimpse of two black metal file cabinets in his A-frame, standing up against the back wall of a walk-in closet she had opened "accidentally" while looking for the bathroom. Both were locked, which could mean anything...or nothing.

Ross meant to have a little peek inside.

Pike had enjoyed her, asked her number, and she'd made one up to pacify him. She calculated that he wouldn't call her back for several days at least. By that time she would already have searched his files, retrieved whatever seemed most useful. None of it would stand in court, without a warrant, which she didn't have a prayer of getting, but there might be something that would put her on another trail, something she could pass along to others, maybe follow up herself if her superiors at ATF refused to help.

Whatever, she couldn't take waiting for the other shoe to drop. If something didn't happen soon, she feared that she would lose it, take her gun and—

Take the gun.

She needed no reminder, given the circumstances. Ross used the same side arm carried by FBI agents for several years, the Smith & Wesson Model 411, an autoloader chambered in .40 caliber—formerly 10 mm—with plenty of stopping power at normal shoot-out range. In fact it would be accurate to say she used it only on the firing range, but the woman told herself that she wasn't afraid to shoot a man—Pike in particular, or any of his goons who were responsible for snuffing out her partner's life.

She hoped it wouldn't come to that, at least today. She was still trying to connect the dots in her own way, find something that would shut down the whole militia operation, instead of simply dropping one or two of those involved. It seemed the least that she could do for Jeff, when he had done so much.

When she was dressed—black turtleneck, black jeans, tough hiking boots, a navy windbreaker to hide the pistol in her waistband—Ross drove her rental car back over Pike's route from their night together. She guessed there would be no one at the A-frame, but she had two stories cooking in her mind in case she was mistaken. If she met someone besides the colonel, she would be a tourist who had lost her way. If Pike showed up, she would be love struck, ditch the gun before he had a chance to see it and persuade him that she simply couldn't wait until he called her back.

It was a risky move, but she had already stepped well beyond the pale as far as regulations were concerned. A simple threat of death meant less to Ross than it would have the week before. So much had changed, in fact, that she was almost looking forward to the danger, some excuse to fight—even to kill—instead of merely sitting on her hands.

She found a hard-rock station on the radio and turned it up, then put her rental car in gear and went to scout the colonel's lair.

IT WAS A DRONE'S JOB, running errands, but Stone didn't mind this time. He needed space, an opportunity to check in with his contact via telephone and time to think about the previous night's developments back at the compound.

Stone had no idea if Lou Doyle was—had been—a federal plant. No one would ever know now that the idiot was dead. For all Stone knew, that business with the money and Belasko's footlocker could have been simple payback for a broken nose and loss of face. It didn't have to mean that Doyle was working for the FBI or ATF. Granted, he could have been, and yet…

The more Stone thought about Belasko in the light of day, the more he worried. There was no good reason for it, nothing he could put his finger on. In fact the new man on the team had done all right so far. He stood his ground in Denver, even when Doyle—or somebody—had tried to take his head off with a bullet, and he had eliminated their pursuers on the getaway. Of course, he hadn't killed the pigs, but that was just as well in retrospect. There was enough heat from the bungled robbery without the whole state of Colorado screaming for their blood because a cop or two got wasted in the line of duty.

But had Doyle been responsible for the snafu? Was he the one who dropped a dime and had the Feds waiting when they made their move? He made a handy scapegoat now that he was dead, unable to defend himself, but what if it were someone else?

Stone didn't care what ultimately happened to the Paul Revere Militia, but he still had work to do inside the group, and getting busted by the Feds—much less gunned down— wasn't part of the plan.

He never spoke directly to his contact on the telephone. There was an answering machine that took his cryptic messages, and on the rare occasions when a meeting was required, he left coordinates, a date and time. His paymaster had never failed to show, had never shown the slightest hint of nerves at being seen with Stone in public.

He was cool, that one, and no mistake.

Stone wondered where he came from—somewhere in the Middle East, that much was obvious—but he wasn't inclined to blow the deal by asking questions. There was too much money on the table, and he needed a retirement fund. If Stone played his cards right, double-checked each move before he made it, this could be his last job.

For a while, at least.

It made him laugh, sometimes, to think about the Paul Reveres. For all their paranoia, fears of being watched and infiltrated by a swarm of federal agents, they had readily accepted him with hardly any background check at all. Deep down Pike and the bulk of his recruits still loved America so much that they were awed by anyone who talked the talk and walked the walk. Unfortunately, for their prospects of success, they were in love with an America that had ceased to exist in the 1950s, maybe even earlier. They saw the crime rates, rising taxes, lagging growth in the economy, illegal aliens arriving by the thousands every week, and longed for an America that used to be—before the welfare state, gay-rights parades, sex education in the schools, race quotas on the job and in the universities. Before small farmers got plowed under in the name of agribusiness.

They made it easy, trying to regain an era that would never come again—unless their precious Yahweh snapped his fingers and reversed the calendar some fifty years or so. The day that happened, Stone would know that it was time to pack it in. Meanwhile he still had work to do.

He made his phone call from a filling station north of Blackfoot and kept it short and sweet. From what he said, his contact could make out that someone had prepared a trap for them in Denver, and that he had narrowly escaped. It was the only solid information Stone possessed, and it would have to do for now.

It had been Pike's idea for Stone to fetch the file cabinets from his A-frame. Why the old man had them there to start with, why he hadn't simply put them in his car when he was there the night before, was anybody's guess. Maybe his mind was going, Alzheimer's or something similar. And then again, perhaps the incident with Doyle had set him thinking, dwelling on the risk that someone might stop by while he was gone and have a look inside those files.

Stone didn't know precisely what those files contained, nor did he care. His job wasn't to spy on Pike and his militia, but to lead them on a series of "adventures," as his sponsor called them, which would agitate the Feds and send successive shock waves through America at large. So far it had been relatively easy, but the game was heating up. The stakes included Stone's own life, and he wasn't prepared to flush it down the toilet for a stranger, even if that stranger paid him very well indeed. A day was coming when he might have to withdraw and cut his losses, but it hadn't happened yet.

Not even close.

Stone saw the car before his own vehicle cleared the tree line, and he slammed on his brakes before he could be glimpsed by anyone inside the A-frame. Pike wasn't expecting any visitors that Stone knew of, which meant he had a prowler on his hands. The good news was, the vehicle in front of him was no police car.

Kids? A nosy neighbor? Stone had no choice but to check it out and see.

He killed the Jimmy's engine, easing the door shut as he climbed out of the vehicle. A moment later he was slinking through the trees, Glock 17 in hand, to scout the A-frame and discover for himself how many trespassers were on the premises.

The car was small—four passengers would probably feel cramped inside it—and there was a rental sticker on the windshield. This was getting better all the time. A rental meant no law-enforcement car pool and, perhaps, nobody waiting for a check-in call. It seemed unlikely that a tourist in the neighborhood of Blackfoot would have found Pike's A-frame, much less stopped to visit, but you never knew these days.

Stone made a circuit of the building, peering through a couple of the windows, glimpsing no one. Finally he reached the door and tried it, felt the knob turn in his hand.

Unlocked.

He stepped inside and left the door wide open, just in case he had to make his exit in a hurry. Moving forward in a crouch, his pistol held in front of him, Stone followed rustling, shuffling sounds along a corridor of sorts until he stood outside an open closet door. A light was on inside the closet, and he saw a woman kneeling with her back turned toward him, riffling through the top drawer of a stubby file cabinet.

Covering the shapely burglar with his pistol, Stone allowed himself a smile and said, "What have we here?"

THE HEAT WAS OFF, as far as Bolan could determine, for his killing of Lou Doyle. The colonel and Chris Stone either believed his story, or they did a decent imitation of credulity. Nothing was said about the lie-detector man from Coeur d'Alene, but Bolan knew there was a chance the guy might turn up unannounced. In that case he would simply have to take his chances on a bust-out, cause as much confusion as he could with limited resources and come back to finish off the job when he could lay his hands on proper tools.

Meanwhile the camp had settled back into a semblance of routine. There had been no memorial for Doyle. Instead, Pike held a shorter ceremony, without Chalmers being present, and informed his troops that an informer had been found and dealt with in the compound. Doyle wasn't named, nor was his absence from the fold explained. Each listener was free to draw his own conclusions, talk it out with friends, whatever...but the message came through loud and clear.

Traitors were an endangered species. They would get no mercy from the patriots they spied on and betrayed. Death was the price of treason—or, at least, of getting caught.

Bolan was on his way to practice at the firing range when he saw Stone leave the compound, riding solo in an off-white Jimmy. It wasn't unusual for members of the team—especially the brass—to come and go, but he couldn't help wondering about Stone's errand, whether it had anything to do with him.

Pike and Stone had checked him out before he was initiated, and his cover would withstand whatever doublechecking they could manage, thanks to Hal Brognola and his support troops at the Farm. Still, Bolan wished he could get down to business, end the waiting and begin the mopping up. It was his specialty, and every moment wasted gave his enemies an edge.

The shooting helped a little. Bolan worked his way

straight through the course, using a silent MP-5 SD-3 set for 3-round bursts. The silhouettes were set to jump at random, switching patterns every pass for three runs straight before they started to repeat themselves. He knew what he was doing, but it still demanded concentration, watching out for the "civilians," capping "bad guys" that included uniformed police in this scenario.

The second time he ran it through, he had an audience. The first two soldiers multiplied to half a dozen, then redoubled, watching Bolan work the angles—dodging, rolling, nailing one target after another. As the Executioner stepped back from the firing line, removing a spent magazine from his weapon, he spotted Rick Guarini in the front row of his audience.

"That shoulder holding up?" he asked.

"It's getting there," Guarini said. "From what I see, somebody's lucky you were loading paint that afternoon instead of hollowpoints."

"Somebody's luck ran out," Bolan said.

"Yeah, I heard. That Lou. I told you he was trouble."

"Used to be."

"Yeah, right." Guarini hesitated, lowering his voice a notch as they walked back together, toward the armory. "I gotta tell you, Mike, not everybody's broken up to see Lou go. In fact I'd say some of us are relieved."

"That so?"

"The word's around that maybe he was running games for ZOG."

"I wouldn't know about that," Bolan said. "He tried to set me up, then pulled a switchblade when I caught him at it. Maybe it was personal for all I know."

"Whatever. You've got friends in camp, is what I'm saying." Once again Guarini hesitated. "But Lou had his cronies, too."

"I'll watch my back, don't worry."

"That's the ticket, man."

Their course had brought them to the compound's armory when Bolan heard an engine revving, glanced back toward the gates and saw Stone returning. He was in a hurry, from the looks of it, driving right up to the colonel's quarters and jumping out of his vehicle. He ran inside, and a moment later he was back with Pike, both men peering through the back-door window, checking out some object on the seat or floorboards.

Pike was livid, angry color blazing in his face. His words to Stone didn't reach Bolan's ears across the intervening distance, but Stone got back in the driver's seat of his vehicle, swung it in a tight U-turn and gunned it back across the open center of the compound toward a barracks on the far north end.

"What's that about?" Bolan asked, trying not to sound too curious.

"Beats me," Guarini said.

They were almost a hundred yards away from Stone when he parked the vehicle a second time and killed the engine, bailed out on the driver's side and opened the back door. The object he removed from the back seat turned out to be a human being—female, with her hands secured behind her back. Guarini whistled softly at the sight, but Bolan felt his blood run cold.

The first time he had seen her, it was dark out, but he had no trouble whatsoever recognizing Agent Ginger Ross.

HER CAPTOR LEFT her clothes on, all except the jacket, which was something to be thankful for—so far. He had relieved her of the pistol, though, and that was in the minus column, big time. And she was seated in a straight-backed wooden chair, with her arms and legs secured with duct tape.

Right now, though, Ginger Ross was concerned about her own survival in the next few hours. The prospects weren't encouraging by any means.

She recognized Pike's head honcho—Stone, his name was—from the briefings back when Jeff was still alive. He'd taped her to the chair while one of his subordinates stood by and kept her covered with a pistol. Then they had left her. No groping, threats, no rough stuff—nothing. That was weird, but Ross thought she understood the theory. They would let her stew awhile, her own imagination conjuring worse terrors than her captors could devise, and maybe she would break down sooner, when they really went to work.

She knew that military men like Pike and Stone would have some nasty tricks for making people talk against their will. Pike had done time in Vietnam, and every postwar college graduate knew all about the VC grillings with electric shocks and water torture, gang rapes, people tossed from helicopters cruising at a thousand feet above the jungle. Okay, maybe she could rule out that one, but there were still enough grim possibilities to make her sweat, and she was feeling absolutely clammy by the time Pike arrived, with Stone in tow.

"We meet again," the colonel said.

"The pleasure's all yours," Ross told him.

"I imagine so." He spent a moment staring at her, venom in his eyes, before he said, "You set me up. I can't hold that against you, in the circumstances—spies do what they do in war, we all know that—but you will understand that I'm required to ask you certain questions."

"I can save us all some time," she said. "The answer is, 'Go fuck yourself.'"

Pike's smile looked strained. Behind him Stone was blank, apparently emotionless. He was the one who would be truly dangerous.

"I like a prisoner with spirit," Pike informed her. "To a point, that is. All soldiers value courage, even in their enemies, but that doesn't prevent them from accomplishing their mission."

"Which, in your case, would be blowing up the federal government and turning the United States into a racist, right-wing funny farm."

"You're misinformed, my dear. While they were teaching you to fuck for Uncle Sam, you must have missed a course or two on the realities of modern politics."

"Enlighten me."

"Unfortunately we don't have the time to fill the gaps in your uneven education. In fact it's your turn to enlighten me."

"Concerning what, pray tell?"

"Let's start with your employers and proceed from there. Your mission, contacts, any special orders, codes—the usual."

"You'd better fetch the rubber hose."

"I think we can improve on that," Pike said.

He nodded to his number two, and Stone moved out of Ross's sight behind the chair. She heard him moving something, and when he came back into view, Stone was pushing a mover's dolly, supporting a heavy truck battery with some kind of jumper cables attached. The giant alligator clips reminded her of fossil skulls, the jaws of some dead predator stripped down to bare essentials.

"As a point of curiosity," Pike said, "do you like rock and roll?"

She saw no way to compromise herself with that one. "Sometimes."

"We don't have any AC/DC for you at the moment," Pike went on, and cocked his head in the direction of the battery. "Just DC, as it happens. Not to worry, though. I guarantee you'll sing a rousing solo by the time we're finished."

"Go to hell," she said.

Pike smiled. "Been there, done that. Shall we begin?"

15

The thing to do was let it go, maintain his cover and let Ginger Ross bear the consequences of meddling in a case from which she had been ordered to withdraw. That much was clear to Bolan, and he knew that any move he made to help her would undo whatever gains he had achieved by taking out Lou Doyle. It was a sucker play, with nothing to be gained and everything to lose, protecting someone who had brought death's shadow on herself.

He knew all that and went ahead regardless.

It was time for Bolan to start to kick ass.

First thing, he checked his vehicle, made sure that it was running and retrieved the sleek Beretta. It would get him started, but he needed more hardware than that to take on a militia. Moving toward the compound's armory, he ran a mental checklist, matching wants against the gear he knew to be available.

There was a guard named David Crowley on the door. His smile showed some confusion at the Executioner's approach. "You going to run the course again?" he asked.

"Guard duty coming up," Bolan replied. "Thought I'd get my weapon now."

The sentry frowned. "The sergeant always handles that, you know?"

A shifting glance around the compound showed no witnesses in sight. If someone had his eyes on Bolan from behind a barracks window, it couldn't be helped.

Instead of answering the sentry's question, Bolan stepped in close and hit him with a forearm shot across the larynx, slamming him back into the door frame with sufficient force to make his eyes glaze over. Bolan didn't know if Crowley was breathing as they crossed the threshold. He dumped the body in a corner, closed the door behind him and began to select hardware for his strike.

He chose a Colt Commando and a bandolier of loaded magazines, slung both across his shoulders, then went on to heft one of the silent SMGs. If possible, he hoped to gain some measure of surprise, and that meant stealth before the roof blew off. However, once it went to hell, he would need firepower to spare, which made him pause and crack a case of hand grenades, affixing half a dozen to his belt.

All done.

The plan was rudimentary at best: grab Ross from the bungalow where she was being held and make it back to Bolan's vehicle, then blast out through the gate and get the hell away from there. It had the virtue of simplicity, but Bolan kept in mind that he was presently outnumbered twenty-five or thirty guns to one. If he managed to retrieve the lady Fed and she had any fight left in her, that would cut the odds in two, but it was still a risky proposition from the jump.

He made it eighty yards between the armory and Ross's prison in a straight line, nearly twice that far if he played cautious, circling around behind the buildings to avoid an open walk across the central compound, carrying his mini-arsenal. The difference in time might well be critical for someone undergoing rough interrogation, but he would be little good to the woman if he got picked off before he reached her.

If he passed unnoticed in the shadows, he could always double-time and make it up that way, while running in the open would be sure to draw attention that he didn't need.

The Executioner made sure that his MP-5 SD-3 had a live round in the chamber, with the safety off, its fire selector set for 3-round bursts. Whatever happened next, his life and Ginger Ross's would be riding on the line.

He left the armory, turned left, then left again and slipped around behind the nearest bungalow, proceeding with long strides toward his appointed rendezvous with death.

CHRIS STONE REMOVED a Benchmade folding knife from the hip pocket of his blue jeans, thumbed it open and stepped closer to the woman in the chair. He knew where to attach the alligator clips, but needed skin to make it work. Since cutting through the duct tape was a no-no, he would slice her clothes instead, beginning with the turtleneck and bra.

He gripped the snug neck of her shirt and brushed the knife against her pale cheek when she tried to bite him. That slowed her down, and he was free to hook the blade inside her clingy neckline, slicing down the middle of the shirt, avoiding contact with her skin. Two more flicks, at the shoulders, and he peeled the cloth back like the skin of an eviscerated animal, leaving the sleeves intact. It was a kinky fashion statement, with her lacy bra exposed, but Stone took care of that with one swipe of his blade between her breasts.

"Jeans, too?" he asked the colonel.

"Might as well," Pike said, "before she starts to sweat."

The jeans were tight. Stone knew that it would take some skill to strip them without drawing blood, but it didn't require a surgeon's touch. And if he nicked the woman once or twice, what of it? All she had to do was answer half a dozen questions, then her life was over. It wasn't as if she needed flawless skin where she was going—to a shallow, unmarked grave.

Too bad, Stone thought. Fear and the creeping chill inside the bungalow had made her nipples stiffen in a show of counterfeit excitement. Personally he would have preferred to take another route with the interrogation, but it wasn't worth the risk entailed by bucking Pike's authority. Not when a high-six-figure payoff might be jeopardized.

He pinched the inseam of her blue jeans on her left leg, just above the duct tape wrapped around her calf, and pierced the denim with the sharp tip of his folding knife. He worked his blade along the tough seam, conscious of her muscles tensed beneath the fabric. He had opened something like an inch of denim, when a sudden blast of gunfire made him jump and prod her with the blade.

"Goddammit!"

Stone was on his feet and moving toward the door, but Pike got there ahead of him. The first shots had been riflefire, full-auto from one of the 5.56 mm weapons that were standard in the compound. Now, as Pike laid one hand on the doorknob, there were more shots from the compound.

Stone reached out to haul the colonel back. "Be careful, sir. We don't know what this means."

"Some numbskull working on the range without a silencer," Pike snapped. "I'll have his ass for disobeying orders and—"

"And if it's not?" Stone asked. "Suppose it's something else?"

"All the more reason we should check it out. Let's go."

Pike didn't wait to see if Stone was with him; he barged through the doorway and was gone. Stone was about to follow the old man when he thought better of it, stopping at the threshold, peering out into the compound. Away to his right, three soldiers were running with rifles in hand toward a target that the mercenary couldn't see. A heartbeat after they were gone, there was more firing, followed closely by the unmistakable concussive sound of a grenade exploding.

That was all Stone had to see and hear. Whatever was happening, it couldn't be explained away as some half-wit forgetting to employ a silenced weapon on the practice range. It was obvious they were in trouble, and if grenades were being tossed around out there, it meant the racket would be audible for miles. Assuming Pike and company could solve the problem in the next few moments, there was still a major risk of hostile neighbors phoning a complaint in to the county sheriff's office, which, in turn, was bound to notify the Feds.

Big trouble.

Between explosions and the sound of automatic-weapons fire, the ATF would have no problem getting warrants. It would take a while, but in the meantime every wasted moment made it more unlikely that he would escape the compound, free and clear. Abandoning his post was risky, too, but there were ways around that problem if he was alive.

And if he wasn't, well, his other problems would be no more critical than two farts in a hurricane.

Of course, it would be helpful if he had a ticket out.

Stone turned and found the woman staring at him with a mix of fear and hatred in her eyes, two raw emotions he could understand from personal experience.

He walked toward her, showing her the knife, and said, "Relax, babe. We'll be going for a little ride."

THE WOMAN LET Stone free her legs before she tried to take him out. He had to give her credit, with the gun and all. A swift kick toward his face and she just might have pulled it off, if he hadn't glanced up in time and seen the action coming in her eyes. The way it was, he blocked the kick with his free hand and grabbed her by the ankle, dragged her from the chair and dumped her on the floor with a resounding thud.

Looming over her, the Glock aimed at her startled face, Stone felt the sense of power he enjoyed so much. In other circumstances he would probably have run with it, decided how to pay her back for her impertinence in ways that would amuse him, but he simply didn't have the time for that right now.

Outside there was a war in progress, and he didn't even want to know who was responsible. If it was something Pike's militiamen could wrap up quickly, they would have finished it already. Clearly it was time for him to take evasive action and review his options, to prevent himself from being bagged at any cost.

"I'm leaving in about one minute," Stone informed the woman. "You can come along, or I can leave you here."

"I'll call a cab," she told him, sitting up and covering her breasts.

"That's not an option," he replied. "I can't have any witnesses. You get my drift?"

She saw where he was going, spent a heartbeat staring at the Glock, then glanced down at her chest. "I can't go anywhere like this," she said, "unless you're headed for a topless club."

Stone was impressed that she retained her sense of humor. Moving toward the nearest wall, he took an OD jacket from a hook and tossed it to her.

"Put that on," he said. When she had done as she was told, he ordered, "Get on your feet and face the wall, both hands behind your back."

It was a risky moment, when she might well make another move, but Stone was ready for her. Coming up behind her, he clamped one hand on her nape and shoved her forward until she was leaning at a forty-five-degree angle, supporting her weight on her forehead, pressed against the wall. Before she knew it, he had snapped the handcuffs on her wrists and used the collar of her baggy jacket as a handle, dragging her upright once more.

"This is the plan," he said, standing close enough that his breath disturbed the hair along her neckline as he spoke. "We're going for a ride. I haven't picked a final destination yet. As long as you're of use to me, you live. The first time you attempt to slow me down, escape, call out for help or any other action that could be construed as hostile to my own best interest, I'll be pleased to kill you. Do we understand each other?''

''All except one thing,'' she said.

''Which is?''

''You've said you can't afford to leave a witness. Why should I believe you'll ever let me go?''

''Good point,'' Stone said. Most hostages wouldn't have thought that far ahead. ''I'm bound for someplace out of the country, where they don't have extradition treaties. Think of yourself as my travel insurance. Once I'm clear, you're no more threat to me. There's no reason I should take you out.''

''And you've got lakefront property in the Sahara Desert that you'd like to sell, I bet.''

''Your choice,'' he told her, raising the Glock until its sights were lined up on her face. ''You've got five seconds to decide.''

''Well, since you put it that way, where's our ride?''

Smart girl.

''I've got the wheels laid by,'' he told her. ''What we need to focus on right now is getting from point A to point B in one piece. There may be friends of yours out there for all I know, but flying bullets don't have any loyalty.''

''I'll remember that.''

''You should. Let's go.''

Stone took her by the arm and steered her toward the door. She didn't struggle with him, moving of her own accord. Stone cracked the door an inch or so and peered outside, looking for enemies. A pall of smoke obscured his vision, drifting from the right.

No problem. Stone had parked his ride off to the left, away from what appeared to be the epicenter of the firefight. They could make it if they got their act together and the woman didn't try to hold him back.

"We're going to the left," Stone said. "I'll show you where. Just keep your head down, and you should be fine, as long as you play fair. Remember, though, your first mistake will also be your last."

"Let's do it," she replied.

And so they did.

IT HAD BEEN PURE bad luck that nearly got him killed and thereby kept him from his destination. Bolan had no more than started toward the bungalow where Ginger Ross was being held, the long way around, when he met Rick Guarini on his way to the latrine. It could have been a casual encounter, but the hardware Bolan carried ruled out any explanation that made sense. Guarini took one look at him and stopped dead in his tracks, mouth turning downward in a frown.

"Hey, Mike, what's going on?"

That sounded casual, but he could almost hear the clamor of alarm bells in Guarini's brain, saw dark eyes shifting left and right in search of an escape hatch.

There was nothing he could say, no time to waste with lies. This was one of Bolan's enemies, potentially his killer, and he dared not hesitate. Another second, and Guarini could be shouting to the others, bringing reinforcements on the run.

Instead, the would-be soldier tried to draw a smallish autoloader from his pocket, snagging it on fabric, cursing as it stuck. He saw death coming for him, and the color drained from his face as if someone had pulled a plug below his belt.

"Bastard!"

The MP-5 SD-3 whispered, three rounds slamming into Guarini's chest. He staggered backward, reeling, going down, but not before his index finger clenched around the little side arm's trigger, pumping two rounds through the fabric of his pants.

The bullets didn't come within a yard of Bolan, but the shots were loud enough to wake the dead. Immediately someone started shouting from the far side of the bungalow that served as Bolan's cover, other voices answering and drawing closer by the moment.

The Executioner had to move, ditch Plan A in a heart-beat, and he didn't hesitate. Instead of sprinting for the bungalow where Ross was confined, he turned to face the sound of voices, moved in that direction, swiveling the Colt Commando on its shoulder sling until he had an automatic weapon in each hand.

Four soldiers were close enough to matter, one of them Jack Cartwright, as he cleared the space between two bungalows. Three of them carried pistols, which were fairly common in the camp. They gaped at Bolan, clearly startled by the sight of him with guns in hand but hesitant to open fire on one of their own. If he could only take advantage of their momentary lapse...

"This way!" he snapped at them. "Guarini's hit. He needs a medic."

"What's...?"

Cartwright saw it coming, tried to dodge and yelled, "Look out!" By then it was too late, the two guns Bolan held already spitting death into the stunned quartet.

He saw Cartwright's pistol coming up, a snarl of animal defiance on the gunner's face, and hosed him with the Colt, a stream of 5.56 mm tumblers ripping through the man's chest and throat. The others jostled one another as they tried to break for cover, screwing up their shots at Bolan while he cut them down.

From that point on, it was no good pretending that he had a prayer of quietly retrieving Ginger Ross. At least two dozen Paul Reveres were in the open compound now, attracted by the shouts and sounds of gunfire, many of them packing side arms, one or two with rifles. It wouldn't be long before the more resourceful of them made a beeline for the armory and brought out the heavy hardware.

No time to waste.

Bolan had need of a diversion, and he needed it right now. The thought translated into instant action, and he left the SMG to dangle from its shoulder sling as he unclipped a fragmentation grenade and yanked the safety pin. The nearest building was a ten-man barracks, situated between Bolan and a group of militiamen moving in his direction. It was unclear whether they had scoped out the situation as yet, but he wasn't inclined to wait to see.

It was an easy pitch from where he stood, through a side window of the barracks building with a crash of glass. Bolan reversed directions, ducking back the way that he had come before the grenade went off like muffled thunder, blowing out the front wall of the barracks in a cloud of smoke and dust.

He came out firing through the smoke cloud, spotting targets in the haze and dropping each in turn. A couple of the gunners were already down and squirming, hit by shrapnel from the blast, and Bolan left them where they were, swept past them in a rush to reach his destination. He was conscious of the numbers running in his head, the doomsday clock about to chime.

How long before his time ran out? No matter. He would do with what he had, and if it didn't get the job done, he would be in no position to complain.

And suddenly it seemed the mountain air was filled with angry hornets, buzzing past his face and overhead. Enough of Pike's militiamen had recognized their danger and its source to pose a threat, returning fire as Bolan fought his way across the compound.

He kept going all the same. To hell with strategy and planning. It was do-or-die, time to go for broke.

The Executioner wouldn't have had it any other way.

ROSS HAD THOUGHT of Mike Belasko when they reached the compound, wondered whether he would notice her, if there was something he could do to help, but she had put such thoughts aside when she was duct taped to the chair.

Abandon hope, all ye who enter here. She was on her own.

She concentrated on the car, putting one foot before the other, wondering if it was worth the risk to take another flying kick at Stone to try to bring him down. A kung-fu expert could have done it easily, but Ross's training in the martial arts was limited to what she learned in the academy: takedowns, disarming moves, the rudiments of self-defense without finesse. It wouldn't be enough to trip him, though; she had to get the Glock away from him, immobilize him somehow, and that would be difficult without the use of either hand.

Two options, then. In one scenario, she took down Stone and broke away, tried running for her life while he was fighting for his balance. Win or lose, she realized, survival was a long shot—longer than the one that he would put between her shoulder blades while she was trying to outrun a bullet.

The alternative was to submit, get in the vehicle—assuming either one of them survived that long—and see what happened next. She didn't have the first idea of who was shooting up the camp or why, except to say with confidence that it wasn't a federal raid. The Bureau or her colleagues from the ATF would have announced themselves with loudspeakers and helicopters circling overhead before it ever came to gunplay. This was something else, and while she didn't mind the thought of Pike's commandos being shot to pieces, she didn't care to join them, either, if she could avoid it.

They were almost to the car, Stone dragging her along, when Ross stumbled and went down on one knee, almost toppling forward on her face. Her captor cursed a blue streak, dragged her to her feet and shoved her toward the car.

"I warned you, dammit! Nothing fancy!"

"I fell down, for Christ's sake! Are you blind, or what?"

"I see just fine," he told her, jabbing the Glock between her shoulder blades. "Believe me when I tell you, at this range I couldn't miss."

"You want to talk or haul ass out of here?" she challenged him.

They reached his vehicle a moment later, the same Jimmy he had used to transport her from Blackfoot to the compound. Stone led her around to the passenger side and opened the door, which had been left unlocked. He shoved her in and reached across her with the shoulder harness, buckling it down by her hip. He remained silent as he stepped back, thumbed the locking switch and closed the door.

Another moment, and he scrambled in behind the wheel, pausing to wedge the Glock between his right leg and the seat cushion before he twisted the ignition key.

Stone backed out the Jimmy from where it had been parked between two bungalows. He glanced in each direction, up and down the compound north and south by Ross's hazy reckoning. When he had shifted into Drive, he cranked the wheel hard to his left and took off toward the gate that she remembered from surveillance of the camp, and from her own arrival ninety minutes earlier. He stood on the accelerator, and she felt the rear tires spinning for a moment, finally digging in, before the vehicle vaulted forward.

She knew she was dead no matter what, then tried to banish that idea before it could take root and make her panic. She was still alive, would have been dead by now if she had forced the point with Stone back in the bungalow. While she was breathing, there was always hope.

She saw Mike Belasko moving through the smoke a heartbeat later, tall and deadly looking in his camouflage fatigues, firing an automatic rifle at a couple of militiamen who never had a chance. They went down, jerking as if they had stepped onto the third rail of a subway track, blood spurting from their wounds. And then, as if on cue, Belasko turned to face the Jimmy, had his weapon raised...and hesitated.

Did he see her, with her face pressed up against the window glass? How could he not? Ross felt hot tears springing to her eyes, hope like a swift punch in the solar plexus, there and gone as Stone sped past Belasko, racing toward the gate. She felt like screaming, but at whom? What would she say?

She didn't even know who Mike Belasko was, much less whom he was working for. He obviously had a bone to pick with the militia, but that didn't mean he was a federal officer, much less her private savior in disguise.

She had to take her last, best shot at Stone next time she got a chance.

Okay.

If that was how it had to be, Ross would act on the assumption that she had nothing to lose.

The gate loomed up before them, closed, unguarded. Stone kept going, plowed right through it with an awful scraping sound that meant the Jimmy had been flayed of paint along both sides. It would look bad on the insurance claim, she thought, and almost laughed aloud at that.

She had to sit tight and bide her time. With nothing to lose, she had nothing to fear.

Except death.

THE GLIMPSE of Ginger Ross and Stone galvanized him. An instant later, he was sprinting for his Blazer across the main width of the compound, bent on giving chase.

The chaos helped a little. With the drifting smoke and general confusion, pockets of militiamen were trading shots with one another, thinking they had met the enemy, uncer-

tain who their adversaries were. The crazy firefights broke
off when they recognized each other, then resumed in other
quarters with a shift of wind, a new direction for the smoke
screen, yet another faceless threat.

Three camou-clad commandos suddenly appeared in
front of Bolan, moving on a hard collision course. He recognized one of them—Hicks, he thought the name was—
and the soldier IDed Bolan almost simultaneously.

"Hey, man," Hicks called out to him, "what is this
shit?"

"Some kind of raid," Bolan said, grateful for the break
and playing to his adversary's paranoia. "ATF, I think, or
maybe FBI. They're coming in from the east side."

He jerked a thumb back toward the far side of the camp,
behind him, where another burst of automatic-weapons fire
rang out, as if in answer to the gesture.

"Where the hell are *you* going?" Hicks asked.

"I'm looking for the colonel," Bolan lied. "Stone sent
me to find out if he's all right."

"We haven't seen him," Hicks said. "Anyway, I'll
catch you later. Let's go, men!"

They moved past Bolan, heading for the fight. It would
have been an easy thing to shoot them in the back, but
Bolan let them go, continuing toward the Blazer.

Another moment put him in the driver's seat, with keys
in hand. The engine caught and held its beat on Bolan's
first attempt. He shifted into gear and powered out of there,
in hot pursuit of Stone and Ginger Ross.

It was a fluke that Colonel Pike appeared in front of him
just then. Bolan couldn't have planned it in a million years,
the old man suddenly right there, two soldiers close behind
him, moving west to east in the direction of the heavy
firing. Pike glanced up in time to see the Blazer bearing
down on him, perhaps with clarity enough to recognize the
man behind the wheel before its fender caught him in the

side and slammed him backward, toppling his two-man honor guard.

A fatal hit? There was no way of knowing, short of doubling back, and Bolan had more pressing matters on his mind. The gates were open when he got there, one side flattened, while the other sagged from twisted hinges. Flecks of bright paint on the gray chain link confirmed that he was on the Jimmy's trail.

Stone had a lead, but not that much of one. Bolan assumed he would be driving like a wild man, set his own pace to accommodate the enemy's and watched his Blazer eating up the unpaved access road.

He glimpsed the Jimmy up ahead, then it vanished as it went into a turn, his view cut off by trees. Had Stone been looking at his rearview mirror in that fraction of a second?

Never mind.

When he got close enough, there would be time to pick his shot, decide which weapon he should use to minimize the risk of wounding Ross. Better not to kill Stone outright, if she didn't have a chance to grab the steering wheel.

He roared into the final straightaway and took his foot off the accelerator instantly, recoiling from the image of the Jimmy parked across the road no more than forty yards in front of him. His heel was on the brake when Stone opened fire, his bullets knocking divots in the Blazer's windshield, shattering the whole thing into glassy pebbles with his third or fourth round.

Bolan ducked, tried to control his skid and wished he had taken time to buckle his shoulder harness as the Blazer struck a tree and died on impact. As it was, the air bag on the driver's side kept him from a fatal injury with the steering column, but his lungs were emptied by the impact.

Seconds later, when he scrambled from the Blazer, he could barely see the Jimmy's brake lights, winking as Stone reached the county highway. A heartbeat later, he turned south and was gone.

The Blazer tried to start when Bolan turned the key, but something banged and rattled underneath the hood—the fan, perhaps, or something else he couldn't do without. He let the disappointment flood him for perhaps five seconds, then dispelled it and and climbed out of the car.

It was a long walk to the nearest town, and he was losing daylight. Looking like grim Death incarnate, Bolan left the car and moved off through the trees.

16

"The Bureau has a SWAT team and forensics cleaning up the property," Brognola said into the scrambled telephone. "They've got some help from ATF—the weapons angle—and a couple of U.S. attorneys were assigned to make the case. The dragnet's out for the Paul Reveres right now. State forces are cooperating for the most part."

Bolan's voice came back at him from somewhere on the far side of the Rockies. "How many in custody so far?"

Brognola shuffled notes and faxes. "Let me see. It looks like twelve...no, make that thirteen at last count. Plus one dead. Guy by the name of Eric Hicks. He shot a trooper on a traffic stop at Soda Springs. Highway patrol chased him for six or seven miles and ran him off the road into a canyon. Broken neck, they tell me."

There was silence on the other end. Brognola felt obliged to fill the void with words, as if permitting silence to disrupt their conversation would produce some natural catastrophe.

"You heard about the colonel, I suppose," he said.

"No, what about him?"

"Couple of his soldiers dropped him at the hospital in Blackfoot. Tried to tell the duty nurse he'd fallen off a horse, but doctors say it looks more like a hit-and-run. The broken bones include his pelvis, both legs, half a dozen ribs, a hairline fracture of the skull."

"But he's alive?"

"Oh, sure," Brognola said. "A tough old bird like that, he's hard to kill."

"I see that."

"Say, about that other thing..." Brognola hesitated, hating to go on, but the request had come through channels, and he had to pass it on. "The brass at ATF still hasn't heard from Ginger Ross, and they were wondering—"

"She's in the bag," Bolan said. "Stone got hold of her. I don't know how. We didn't have a chance to talk. He took her with him when he split."

Brognola closed his eyes and waited for the sour taste to fade. A fellow officer in peril, and it was ten to one she was already dead. No matter how often he faced the situation, read about it in the papers, went to the official funerals, it never changed—the burning in his gut, a feeling as if he had swallowed something vile and it was fighting to escape.

"I'm sorry," he told Bolan. There was nothing else to say.

"It could be that she's still alive," the Executioner replied.

That much was true. The woman *could* be alive, but for how long? What difference did it make when they had no idea of where Chris Stone was headed or how he planned to get there?

"They found Stone's car in Pocatello," he told Bolan. "I was coming to that next. He dumped it in the airport's long-term parking lot. One of their rent-a-cops picked up on the description, and we caught a lucky break. Still, it could be a while before we get reports on stolen vehicles for a new bulletin. Somebody takes off for a weekend—or a week—and we won't know their wheels are gone until they know it, right?"

"He could be anywhere by then."

"My point exactly," Brognola said. "In the circumstances, ATF won't be expecting any further contact with their missing agent. They're allowing for a decent interval, in case some kind of miracle occurs, but otherwise they've got her down as KIA.''

"They wrote her off.'' It didn't come out sounding like a question.

"We discussed the odds that Stone might let her go,'' Brognola said. "I tried to sound encouraging, but nobody was buying it. Including me.''

"Suppose there was a way to bring her back.'' Once again Bolan wasn't asking. It was more as if he was talking to himself.

"The brass would be relieved, I'm sure. Save them the money on a full-dress funeral, anyway.''

"This isn't finished,'' Bolan told him.

"It may as well be. Pike's definitely looking at some federal-prison time, on weapons counts if nothing else. They'll probably run Stone this weekend on 'America's Most Wanted.' It's a wrap.''

"Not yet,'' Bolan said, standing firm. "Stone's smarter than the Bureau gives him credit for, and he's still got a network standing by to help him. There are active Paul Revere Militia members in eleven states, and that's not counting their associates in other groups across the country, up through parts of Canada.''

"You can't clean up the whole right wing,'' Brognola told him.

"That's not the plan. But I started out to do a job, and it's not finished yet.''

"So, what's your next move, then?''

"You'll know as soon as I do,'' the soldier stated, and broke the link.

Brognola couldn't help but frown as he replaced the telephone receiver in its cradle. It was no good arguing with Bolan when the big guy had his mind made up; that much he knew from personal experience. He knew the rules, knew when to bend them, when to throw them out the window and start making up a list of new ones as he went along. And it had always worked out well enough.

So far.

This time Brognola wondered if his old friend weren't biting off too much. He understood how Bolan's mind worked, knew that he took any failure as a personal affront. In this case, with a missing agent still in jeopardy, Brognola was afraid that Bolan might go overboard in an attempt to clean the whole mess up.

One thing was certain, though. Now that the Executioner had ditched his infiltrator's guise and had returned to normal combat mode, there would be hell to pay. The big Fed almost felt a pang of sympathy for Bolan's targets.

Almost, but not quite.

Whatever happened next, the men who had declared war on the government of the United States had brought it on themselves. Brognola hoped they were prepared to get a taste of hell on earth, because the cleansing fire was on its way.

Ready or not.

THE FIRST CALL Chris Stone placed was to his sponsor, making sure to beat the early media reports from Idaho. He wanted his own version of events to be the first his contact heard, a means of mitigating the disaster and diverting any blame from Stone. He still had no idea who was responsible for the attack, but with a federal spy locked in the trunk of the gray BMW he had stolen from the Pocatello airport parking lot, it was a damn sight easier to sell his patron on the notion of a raid by agents of the FBI or ATF.

His sponsor wasn't happy, but Stone finally convinced him that their operation, while delayed, wasn't derailed. Not yet. Stone had a few more aces up his sleeve, more contacts in the movement who would help him out if they knew what was good for them. In fact the raid on Pike's compound might even be a good thing for the master plan, if it received sufficient media attention, spreading paranoia in the proper quarters.

All things come to those who wait.

He didn't feel like waiting any longer to get moving, though. Not with the federal bloodhounds sniffing on his trail. It wouldn't take them long to find the Jimmy, somewhat longer to decide what he was driving now. Before they put it all together, Stone intended to be safely out of U.S. jurisdiction with his hostage, well beyond the reach of Uncle Sam's long arm.

He made the second call from Flagstaff, Arizona, shortly after 2:00 a.m. His party picked up on the third ring, wide-awake despite the hour, and they spoke in cryptic phrases, using code that Stone himself had helped devise for such occasions. By the time he cradled the receiver, everything was set.

Now all he had to do was get across the border with his hostage undetected.

Easy.

He would assume the Feds were hunting him by now, that they would know his face and name from various surveillance records. At the very least they would be after him for questioning about the firefight at the compound. Beyond that the charges would be anybody's guess. Stone had been extracareful with his fingerprints and other evidence on missions where he led a strike team in the field, but it was possible that someone in the camp would break and spill his guts when the interrogators went to work. There was a world of difference between weapons charges and the rest of it, but Stone didn't intend to serve a day of time for anything if he could help it.

And he could. The mercenary was convinced of that.

Stone knew he couldn't drive all day through Arizona's desert and across the border with his hostage in the BMW's trunk. It would be fatal for the woman, and while he wasn't concerned about her health in any abstract terms, a corpse was worse than useless to him if he needed to negotiate with the authorities somewhere along the way. In that event—which he still hoped he could avoid—the woman's only benefit to him would be if she was breathing, fit to speak up for herself and reassure the pigs that she would stay alive as long as they conformed to Stone's wishes.

A quarter-hour short of dawn, Stone pulled off on a nameless, unpaved access road near Prescott Valley, popped the vehicle's trunk and walked back to negotiate with Ginger Ross.

"You comfy there?" he asked her when he had removed her gag.

"Beats flying coach," she told him, still the salty one, with all that she had been through.

"I've been thinking you might get a little warm back here as time goes by."

"Don't tell me you're concerned."

"For number one," Stone said. "You're useless to me dead. If that's your choice on how to go, let's get it over with right now."

She stared back at him, trying to decide if he was serious, and had no reason to believe that he was joking. Any small doubt in her mind was banished when he drew the Glock from underneath his windbreaker.

"So, what's it going to be?" he asked.

"I haven't heard my choices, yet," she said.

"Plan A, you ride up front with me, enjoy the air-conditioning. Play nice and keep your mouth shut if we're stopped for any reason."

"And Plan B?" As if she didn't know.

"I dig a hole right now and leave you here."

"I guess I'll ride up front."

He helped her from the trunk and cut the duct tape that secured her ankles, leading her around to the vehicle's passenger side and opening her door before he reached into his pocket for the handcuff key.

"Get in."

The woman did as she was told, ru̶̶̶̶. Stone crouched beside her, watching her ̶̶̶̶ move in the direction of his eyes. Before she ̶̶̶ he was doing, he had snapped one cuff around her s̶̶̶ ankle, with the other locked around the steel frame of the seat, concealed from anyone outside the car once he had closed the door. In doing so, he also used the BMW's child-proof locking system that would keep her door from opening from the inside. She glared at Stone as he slid in behind the wheel, but he could take her dirty looks all day as long as she behaved herself.

"I plan to drive the limit and obey all other laws that I'm aware of during the remainder of our trip," he said. "We shouldn't have a problem with the cops, but we'll be forced to stop a couple times for gas, at least, and there's the border crossing to consider. You'll be tempted to escape or call for help at several points along the way. In fact I wouldn't blame you if you tried. But know this, going in— I *will* waste you and anyone who tries to help you. Maybe they'll get me, but you will die, and you won't be alone. So think about the people you protect and serve before you make your move, all right?"

Ross remained silent, but her eyes said everything he had to hear. She recognized his threat for what it was: a promise from a man who had damn little left to lose and no compunctions whatsoever when it came to spilling human blood. It was enough for now. And at the far end of his journey, she would be expendable again.

Stone put the vehicle into gear and made his way back to the highway, headed south toward Mexico.

THE PONTIAC WAS WAITING for Bolan right where Brognola had promised it would be—in a strip mall in Idaho Falls. The Executioner dropped his rental car and shifted his heavy duffel bags from one ride to the other.

...ents later he was on his way.

He hadn't cleared the next phase of his operation with the big Fed, other than to let him know he wasn't finished with the mission yet. Brognola would have been content to call him off at that point, but he couldn't let it go. There were too many loose ends flapping in the breeze—from Stone's escape with Ginger Ross, to all the units of the Paul Revere Militia that remained unscathed from Bolan's blitz in Idaho.

He cherished no illusion of his own ability to shut down the outfit completely, much less banish the phenomenon in all its guises nationwide. That task would fall to law enforcement, legislators and a small army of sociologists before it was completed. Bolan's job was limited to the specific goal of isolating and defusing what had grown into a public menace, stripping Pike and company of their potential for unleashing terror on the public in America.

And he still had some work to do in that regard.

It might be nice, he thought, to start off with a visit to the hospital in Pocatello. Pike was under guard, and getting in to see him wouldn't be the easiest approach to finding out where Chris Stone might have gone with Ginger Ross, but it was worth a try. And failing that, he would devise some other angle of attack to put him on the mercenary's trail. Along the way, he would roll up as many of the Paul Reveres as he was able, teaching them that there was more to waging war than simply practicing with guns and robbing banks in their spare time.

For all their talk about repression and the great conspiracy in Washington, domestic terrorists of the far right had enjoyed a chilling run of luck the past few years. Twenty-three black churches had been burned by arsonists in seven Southern states, with more than half of those unsolved. There had been fifteen hundred violent incidents at clinics offering abortions, with a handful of convictions on the books. Innumerable other incidents showed up in statistics

"Get in."

The woman did as she was told, rubbing her wrists as Stone crouched beside her, watching her hands for any move in the direction of his eyes. Before she knew what he was doing, he had snapped one cuff around her slender ankle, with the other locked around the steel frame of the seat, concealed from anyone outside the car once he had closed the door. In doing so, he also used the BMW's child-proof locking system that would keep her door from opening from the inside. She glared at Stone as he slid in behind the wheel, but he could take her dirty looks all day as long as she behaved herself.

"I plan to drive the limit and obey all other laws that I'm aware of during the remainder of our trip," he said. "We shouldn't have a problem with the cops, but we'll be forced to stop a couple times for gas, at least, and there's the border crossing to consider. You'll be tempted to escape or call for help at several points along the way. In fact I wouldn't blame you if you tried. But know this, going in— I *will* waste you and anyone who tries to help you. Maybe they'll get me, but you will die, and you won't be alone. So think about the people you protect and serve before you make your move, all right?"

Ross remained silent, but her eyes said everything he had to hear. She recognized his threat for what it was: a promise from a man who had damn little left to lose and no compunctions whatsoever when it came to spilling human blood. It was enough for now. And at the far end of his journey, she would be expendable again.

Stone put the vehicle into gear and made his way back to the highway, headed south toward Mexico.

THE PONTIAC WAS WAITING for Bolan right where Brognola had promised it would be—in a strip mall in Idaho Falls. The Executioner dropped his rental car and shifted his heavy duffel bags from one ride to the other.

Moments later he was on his way.

He hadn't cleared the next phase of his operation with the big Fed, other than to let him know he wasn't finished with the mission yet. Brognola would have been content to call him off at that point, but he couldn't let it go. There were too many loose ends flapping in the breeze—from Stone's escape with Ginger Ross, to all the units of the Paul Revere Militia that remained unscathed from Bolan's blitz in Idaho.

He cherished no illusion of his own ability to shut down the outfit completely, much less banish the phenomenon in all its guises nationwide. That task would fall to law enforcement, legislators and a small army of sociologists before it was completed. Bolan's job was limited to the specific goal of isolating and defusing what had grown into a public menace, stripping Pike and company of their potential for unleashing terror on the public in America.

And he still had some work to do in that regard.

It might be nice, he thought, to start off with a visit to the hospital in Pocatello. Pike was under guard, and getting in to see him wouldn't be the easiest approach to finding out where Chris Stone might have gone with Ginger Ross, but it was worth a try. And failing that, he would devise some other angle of attack to put him on the mercenary's trail. Along the way, he would roll up as many of the Paul Reveres as he was able, teaching them that there was more to waging war than simply practicing with guns and robbing banks in their spare time.

For all their talk about repression and the great conspiracy in Washington, domestic terrorists of the far right had enjoyed a chilling run of luck the past few years. Twenty-three black churches had been burned by arsonists in seven Southern states, with more than half of those unsolved. There had been fifteen hundred violent incidents at clinics offering abortions, with a handful of convictions on the books. Innumerable other incidents showed up in statistics as a twenty-five percent increase in hate crimes over the previous year's figures.

It was time to turn that trend around, if only to a limited degree. The Executioner had it within his power to repay one group of terrorists in kind, and he wasn't about to pass it up.

The woman was another issue altogether. Bolan felt no personal responsibility for her abduction and knew there had been nothing that he could have done to save her, short of blowing his own cover on the night they met and dragging her by force to her superiors. In that case, what would he have gained?

The Denver raid would certainly have gone down unopposed, with loss of loot and life that he could only guess at. Colonel Pike wouldn't be in the hospital right now; Lou Doyle and others of his ilk would still be plotting crimes and staging forays from their base in Idaho.

If nothing else, he could draw consolation from the fact that he had stalled the Paul Revere Militia, left its leadership in disarray. That had to be a plus on any scale.

Still, Bolan felt compelled to help Ginger Ross, if he could. Perhaps it was a weakness in his character, preventing him from focusing with single-minded purpose on the task at hand, but he didn't believe so. With the colonel sidelined, maybe even dying, Chris Stone was his heir apparent, standing first in line to take control of the militia and continue its campaign against America. And since the recent spate of raids apparently owed more to Stone's initiative than Pike's strategic acumen, he could turn out to be a more aggressive leader than the old man he replaced.

Which made him much more dangerous.

Daybreak was lighting the horizon as Mack Bolan turned his Pontiac toward Pocatello, running south on Interstate 15. The colonel didn't know it yet, but Bolan was about to visit him and test his bedside manner. After that, well, he would have to wait and see.

To Bolan's left the eastern skyline was a vista etched in blood.

The Executioner was blitzing on.

* * * * *

Don't miss Executioner #223,
HOUR OF CONFLICT, Volume II in the exciting
AMERICAN TRILOGY.

Take
4 explosive books
plus a
mystery bonus
FREE

Mail to: Gold Eagle Reader Service
3010 Walden Ave.
P.O. Box 1394
Buffalo, NY 14240-1394

YEAH! Rush me 4 FREE Gold Eagle novels and my FREE mystery gift.
Then send me 4 brand-new novels every other month as they come off
the presses. Bill me at the low price of just $15.80* for each shipment—
a saving of 15% off the cover prices for all four books! There is NO extra
charge for postage and handling! There is no minimum number of books I
must buy. I can always cancel at any time simply by returning a shipment
at your cost or by returning any shipping statement marked "cancel." Even
if I never buy another book from Gold Eagle, the 4 free books and surprise
gift are mine to keep forever.

164 BPM A3U3

Name	(PLEASE PRINT)
Address	Apt. No.
City	State	Zip

Signature (if under 18, parent or guardian must sign)

* Terms and prices subject to change without notice. Sales tax applicable in
  NY. This offer is limited to one order per household and not valid to
  present subscribers. Offer not available in Canada.

AC-96

From the creator of Deathlands comes...

OUTLANDERS™

An all-new series by James Axler!

Enter the future—a postholocaust world where the struggle between the classes takes on a whole new reality...where the misery of the final conflagration gives way to a promise of a new beginning...and where the inhabitants of the entire planet find themselves facing a new, all-powerful and alien enemy....

Available this June
wherever Gold Eagle books are sold.

OUT-G